CADENCE CREEK COWBOYS

They're the rough Diamonds of the West…

Sam and Ty Diamond—*trouble is these two cowboys' middle name. With chips on their shoulders the size of hay bales, these rough and rugged men think they need a woman like they need a lame horse. Little do they know…*

Don't miss any of the action in Cadence Creek!

Sam's story, **The Last Real Cowboy** is out in May 2012

With a tip of his Stetson and a lazy smile, Sam Diamond can charm anyone. Except prickly Angela Beck…

Ty's story, **The Rebel Rancher**—*available in June 2012*

Ty Diamond isn't exactly known for his mild reputation. But if he wants to be with Clara Ferguson, he's going to have to show her his gentle side.…

Dear Reader,

Welcome to Cadence Creek—home of the sprawling
Diamondback Ranch and two very sexy men: Sam
Diamond, rancher, and his cousin Ty, a real down-to-his-
boots cowboy. These two bachelors need two good women
to make them settle down, and I've got just the pair. These
girls may come with baggage, but they're made of strong,
resilient stuff. Angela Beck is a social worker on a mission,
and Clara Ferguson's a sweet, nurturing soul looking for a
place to call home.

It all starts with the launch of Butterfly House, a special
women's shelter for victims of abuse. Angela won't let
anyone stand in the way of her plans—not even Sam
Diamond, who saunters into a board meeting with a
devilish smile. She and Sam don't exactly see eye to eye.
But, as we all know, things are rarely as simple as they
seem. Turns out Sam is exactly the kind of man Angela
needs—and Angela is the woman he's been waiting for his
whole life.

I loved writing this story from start to finish, and I hope
you enjoy it too. And don't forget to look for Ty and
Clara's story, coming in July!

I love hearing from readers—you can find me at my
website, www.donnaalward.com.

Until then—happy reading!

Donna

DONNA ALWARD

The Last Real Cowboy

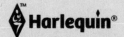

TORONTO NEW YORK LONDON
AMSTERDAM PARIS SYDNEY HAMBURG
STOCKHOLM ATHENS TOKYO MILAN MADRID
PRAGUE WARSAW BUDAPEST AUCKLAND

Recycling programs
for this product may
not exist in your area.

ISBN-13: 978-0-373-74176-2

THE LAST REAL COWBOY

First North American Publication 2012

www.Harlequin.com

Printed in U.S.A.

A busy wife and mother of three (two daughters and the family dog), **Donna Alward** believes hers is the best job in the world: a combination of stay-at-home mom and romance novelist. An avid reader since childhood, Donna always made up her own stories. She completed her arts degree in English literature in 1994, but it wasn't until 2001 that she penned her first full-length novel and found herself hooked on writing romance. In 2006 she sold her first manuscript, and now writes warm, emotional stories for Harlequin Romance.

In her new home office in Nova Scotia, Donna loves being back on the east coast of Canada after nearly twelve years in Alberta, where her career began, writing about cowboys and the West. Donna's debut romance, *Hired by the Cowboy,* was awarded the Booksellers Best Award in 2008 for Best Traditional Romance.

With the Atlantic Ocean only minutes from her doorstep, Donna has found a fresh take on life and promises even more great romances in the near future!

Donna loves to hear from readers. You can contact her through her website at www.donnaalward.com, her page at www.myspace.com/dalward, or through her publisher.

Books by Donna Alward

HOW A COWBOY STOLE HER HEART
A FAMILY FOR THE RUGGED RANCHER
HONEYMOON WITH THE RANCHER
PROUD RANCHER, PRECIOUS BUNDLE

Other titles by this author available in ebook format.

To Jayne, who rescued a very special kitty. And to Chippie—truly one of a kind.

CHAPTER ONE

ANGELA Beck tapped her fingers against the board-room table and frowned. The seat across from her was noticeably empty and she grew more irritated by the moment. They'd held things up long enough, though why Molly Diamond was running so very late was a mystery. Molly was usually right on time.

"Angela, we really can't hold off any longer." Charles Spring, the President of the Butterfly Foundation board, folded his hands and looked down the table at her, his gray eyes stern over the rims of his glasses. "We need to get started."

Charles had graciously agreed to let the foundation meet in the boardroom of his oil and gas company's headquarters. It meant a drive into Edmonton, but Angela knew it was easier for her to commute than for the entire volunteer board to drive to Cadence Creek for a meeting. As a result she'd put together a list of things she needed for the renovations, determined to make the most of the trip. She didn't have any time to waste if she wanted to make her projected opening date.

"I know." Angela forced a smile and made herself remember that every person in the room was volunteering their time. She was the only one drawing a salary from the foundation. The reminder was enough to ensure her patience. The shelter was her dream, but success relied on a lot of people—people who didn't have this project as their top priority the way she did. She couldn't afford to alienate any of them—she'd come too far and invested too much.

"I'll call the meeting to order, then, at 2:18."

For an hour the board members discussed the latest fundraising campaign; Angela outlined the latest PR push and upcoming open house, adding her input to the proposed operating budget and counseling services she'd organized for residents of Butterfly House. She'd thought she'd worked long hours before as a social worker for the province, but that was nothing compared to her days lately, especially as she was a staff of exactly one.

"And now," she said, "I wanted to bring up the suggestion that we hire some short-term help for the minor renovations still needed to the house."

Charles tapped his lip and looked over at the board treasurer, a graying woman with glasses and a stern demeanor. "Iris?"

"Leave it with me," she suggested. "But don't

get your hopes up. The budget is already stretched. What's allocated is barely going to cover the cost of materials. Start adding in labor costs and I start seeing red ink."

"Perhaps if we can get more donations..." Soliciting sponsors was definitely not Angela's favorite part of the job; she hated feeling like the center of attention and preferred to be behind the scenes. But it had to be done and so she did it—with a smile and an eye on the big picture.

The talk then turned to drafting up letters requesting sponsorship. Angela pinched the bridge of her nose. The place needed paint and window coverings and the floor in the living room was in dire need of replacement. Who would come good for all of that?

She straightened her back. She would do it, somehow. She was thrilled that her vision was becoming a reality and it was worth the long hours, the elbow grease and the worry. It would be better when the house was actually ready for residents. In its present state it looked the way she felt—tired and droopy. She'd make it right if she had to do it all herself.

They were down to the last item on the meeting agenda when the door opened and *he* sauntered in. Sam Diamond needed no introduction, Angela thought with disdain. *Everyone* knew who he was. She resolved to keep her expression bland as she looked up, wondering why on earth Sam had shown up instead of his mother, Molly, the Diamond family representative to the board.

Sam turned a slow smile on the group and Angela clenched her teeth. He was going to be trouble—with a capital *T*. She'd known it from the first moment he'd sidled up to her at the Butterfly House fundraiser and had asked in his smooth, deep voice, "Have we met?" Her tongue had tangled in her throat and she'd hesitated, feeling stupid and predictable as a purely feminine reaction warred with her usual timidity when it came to dealing with members of the opposite sex—especially in social situations. Well, maybe he'd had her at a disadvantage during their first meeting, but she'd kept the upper hand in the end and she would today, too. She was far more comfortable in a meeting room than at a cocktail party.

But she'd have to do it delicately. His family had made Butterfly House possible, and it wouldn't do to bite the hand that was feeding her project.

"Mr. Diamond." Charles lifted his head and offered a wide smile. "I'm afraid we started without you."

Started without him? Angela silently fumed. He was over an hour late and had just walked in as though he had all the time in the world! And Charles Spring…she felt her muscles tense. Old boys' club, indeed. Spring might frown at her over his glasses, but to Diamond he was as sweet as her mother's chocolate silk pie!

"I got held up." Sam gave the board a wide, charming smile and removed his hat. "I hope I didn't inconvenience anyone."

"Not at all! There's always time for the foundation's biggest supporter." Heads around the table nodded. Sam shook Charles's hand and then put his thumbs in his pockets.

"I didn't realize I'd be in the company of such lovely ladies," he drawled, popping just the hint of a dimple. Angela swore that she could hear the sighs from three of the board members old enough to be Sam's mother. "I would have made a better effort to be here earlier."

Angela thought she might be sick from all the flattery stuffing up the room. Where was Molly? Why had Sam come in her stead?

"I do hope your mother's okay," Angela said clearly. She took off her reading glasses and put them down on the table. Sam pulled out his chair and met her gaze as he took a seat. Recognition flared in his eyes for a moment, then cleared as if they were perfectly polite strangers.

"She's fine, why do you ask?"

There was an edge to his voice and Angela didn't like it. Maybe he was still nursing a bit of hurt pride where she was concerned. She blinked. Men like Sam Diamond weren't used to being refused. Especially when they bought a lady a drink and told her she was a pretty little thing.

She'd simply said, "No, thank you." It was only afterward that she'd realized that she'd given a Diamond—a pillar of the community—his walking papers. It put her in an awkward position. She needed his family's support.

She ignored the uneasy glances from the board members and pasted on a cool smile. "Molly hasn't missed a meeting yet. She's been so supportive of the foundation. So I'm a bit surprised to see you here today, Mr. Diamond."

Dark eyes met hers, challenging. "And you are?"

Oh, the nerve! He knew exactly who she was. She could see by the gleam in his eye that it was a deliberate cut, intended to throw her off her stride. She lifted her chin and rose to the challenge. "Executive Director of Butterfly House, Angela Beck."

"You obviously didn't receive my message. I called this morning."

And this morning she'd been outside chasing Morris around, trying to get the infernal creature indoors before she had to race into Edmonton. She hadn't stopped to check messages. She resisted the urge to bite down on her lip. She wasn't feeling quite as in charge as she'd like. She was well aware that the Diamond family had a place on the board; after all, they'd donated the building and land for Butterfly House and promised an annual donation toward maintaining the facility. Which was all down to Molly's generosity, she knew. The younger Diamond had a reputation that preceded him and it wasn't all favorable. The fact that he'd tried his charms on her only made it more awkward. Maybe the deed was already signed, but without the continuing support the program would die a quick death unless she could find another sponsor with deep pockets.

"I'm so sorry, I didn't receive it. I've been in the city for several hours already."

Angela was aware that every pair of eyes were on the two of them and that everyone seemed to be holding their breath. Everyone knew Sam. He was a big man, with big money and a big ego. Most of the residents spoke of him as if he were a god. Men respected him and women wanted him—until he trampled on their affections. She'd had her ears filled about that already.

But Angela could see the appeal. He was over six feet in his boots, sexy as sin and looking scrumptious in jeans and a shirt with a sport jacket thrown over top as a concession to business attire. Paired with his unassailable confidence, he made quite the package.

Just because she could understand the attraction did not mean she was interested, though. He was too… Well, he was too everything. She'd known it from the moment he'd tipped his hat and looked down at her with his bedroom eyes. And after she'd refused his overtures, he'd gotten this little half smile. "Do you know who I am?" he'd asked. Clearly she hadn't. But she did now. They both knew exactly who had the upper hand—and he was enjoying it.

How kind, gentle Molly Diamond had spawned such an egomaniac was beyond her. Did he really think his transparent charm would work on her now when it hadn't the first time?

"My mother won't be attending any board meetings for the foreseeable future. My father suffered a stroke last week and she'll be looking after him for the time being. She requested I sit on the board in her place."

Oh, brother. Sympathy for the lovely Molly and her husband Virgil warred with annoyance at the turn of events. Angela and Molly had hit it off from the start, and she'd so looked forward to talking things over with the older, friendly woman. Molly had insisted that she'd love to be involved with turning the house into a real home and had even helped plan the upcoming open house. Angela couldn't imagine Sam helping with those sorts of things. Undoubtedly his impression of "service to the community" was throwing money at it, then smiling and shaking a few hands and feeling proud of himself.

"I hadn't heard." Angela forced herself to meet

his gaze. "I'm very sorry about your dad, Mr. Diamond. Please tell Molly that if she needs anything to give me a shout."

"Thank you."

But the words came out coolly, without the warm flirtatious charm he'd used on the other board members. Great. It seemed his pride was still smarting from her response that night. His question—*Do you know who I am?*—had struck a nerve and made her so defensive that goose bumps had popped up over her arms. "Should I?" she'd answered, looking over her shoulder as she walked away. Her insides had been trembling, but she'd covered it well. She was done letting domineering men run roughshod over her.

She'd utterly alienated Sam and she'd done it in front of the board. He turned his head away now, effectively ending the conversation. And why wouldn't he? She'd been prickly as a cactus. Both times they'd met.

Charles wrapped up the meeting, but before he adjourned he smiled at Sam.

"I'm sure Angela would be happy to fill in the gaps, Sam. She knows more about the project than anyone."

Angela felt the blood rush to her face as Sam's gaze settled on her again. "Of course," she murmured. She would just have to suck it up. What was important was getting Butterfly House off the ground no matter how often she had to smile. Maybe Sam wouldn't even be interested in the details and this would be short and relatively painless.

She could afford a few minutes as long as she could make it to the hardware store in time to pick up her supplies. By the time she finished running her errands, it would be evening before she returned to Cadence Creek. Her whole day would be gone with little accomplished.

The meeting adjourned and the board members filtered out of the room. Sam pushed back his chair just far enough that he could cross an ankle over his knee. Angela organized her papers, avoiding Sam's penetrating gaze as long as possible. Finally she put her pen atop the stack and folded her hands. She looked up and into his stupidly handsome face. "Shall I bring you up to speed, then? Or will you be on your way?"

Sam forced himself to stay relaxed. Lordy, this Ms. Beck was a piece of work. She looked as though she had a perennial stick up her posterior and she clearly didn't approve of him any more now than she had two weeks ago when he'd offered to buy her a drink and she'd flatly refused, looking at him like he was dirt beneath her heel. Which was of no great importance. He didn't need her to like him. In fact, he didn't need anything from her. She needed him, especially now that his mother was otherwise occupied.

He ignored the shaft of fear and concern that weighed him down when he thought of his father and focused instead on the budget in front of him. He was only here because his mother had asked and he couldn't say no to her. Especially not now. In his mind, today's meeting was supposed to be a token appearance and then he could be on his way attending to more important matters.

Instead he found himself sticking around. Aggravating Miss Prim and Proper was a side benefit he hadn't anticipated, and it took his mind off the troubles at home.

"By all means," he said slowly, letting a grin crawl up his cheek purely to irritate her. "Educate me."

Damned if she didn't blush, he thought with some satisfaction. He tilted his head, studying her. Pretty, he decided, or she could be if she let her hair down a little. Now, as it had been at the fundraiser, it was pulled back into a somewhat severe twist, with only a few nearly black strands rebelling by her ears. Her eyes were a stunning color, too, a sort of greeny-aqua that he'd never seen before and he wondered if she wore tinted contacts. As he watched, she put her glasses back on—armor. He recognized the gesture. He was the same way with his hat.

"Is your father going to be all right?" she asked quietly, surprising him. He'd expected facts and figures from Miss Neat and Tidy.

"I think so," he replied honestly. "He's home from the hospital and Mom insists on nursing him herself. Since he requires round-the-clock care, something had to give in her schedule. Your foundation was it."

"Of course. Please give her my best and tell her not to worry about a thing."

Sam uncrossed his legs and leaned forward, resting his elbows on the table. "Let me be honest, Ms. Beck. I don't want to be here. With my dad sick, the running of Diamondback Ranch falls solely to me. I don't have time to sit on charity boards and shake hands, okay? All I'm concerned about is the responsible management of the foundation so my mother's donation is held to a...certain standard."

She looked like she'd just sucked on a lemon. "The Diamonds won't be associated with anything substandard," she replied sharply. "I get it, Mr. Diamond."

She made it sound as though it was a bad thing. Four generations had gone into making Diamond-back what it was—the biggest and best ranch in the county. The standards set by his ancestors were a lot to live up to. And it wasn't just the responsibility of taking the ranch into the future that he carried on his back. Lord knew he loved his mother, but at age thirty-seven he was getting tired of the question of when he was going to provide a fifth generation. When the hell did he have time? His father was seventy-two, his mother in her late sixties. The ranch was bigger than ever and facing new challenges every day. His latest idea—making Diamondback more environmentally friendly—was taking up the rest of his waking hours. And now, with his father being so ill, it made him think about what would happen to Diamondback. To the family. He rubbed a hand over his mouth. Good Lord. Now he was starting to think like his mother. Men weren't supposed to have biological clocks, were they? So why did he suddenly hear ticking?

Now his mother had lassoed him into sitting on this silly board because the Diamonds had donated some land and a house for Miss Goody Two-Shoes to turn into a women's shelter. And he had said yes because Molly had looked very tired and worried and family was important. He didn't plan on being actively involved. He'd write a damned check and keep his hands off.

"Look, we provided the location. What more do you want?"

He hadn't thought it was possible that she would sit up any straighter but she did—her spine ramrod-stiff as her nostrils flared. "The spot on the board was your mother's condition, not mine."

"I know that," he answered, his annoyance growing. What had he done that had made her so hostile? Surely offering a smile and a glass of wine wasn't a crime? And he hadn't meant to be late today. "What I mean is, what in particular do you want from *me*?"

He heard the sharp intake of breath and could nearly hear the words spinning in her head: *not a thing.* Instead she put down her pen, looked him dead in the eye and said, "Your assurance that you won't withdraw funding and that you'll stay out of the way."

"That's blunt."

"Would you rather I was less direct?"

There was a glimmer of respect taking hold in the midst of his irritation. "Not at all. Please. Be honest."

But his invitation was met with silence. He wondered what she wanted to say, what she was holding back.

"Perhaps I should mention the elephant in the room," he suggested. "The fundraiser."

"What about it?"

But now he heard it—a tiny wobble, the smallest bit of uncertainty. "You really didn't know who I was?"

"And that surprises you, doesn't it? Because *everyone* knows Sam Diamond."

He raised an eyebrow at her sarcastic tone. "Frankly, in this area? Yes."

"You really do have an inflated ego."

Sam chuckled. "Are you trying to hurt my feelings, Ms. Beck? Look, you passed up the opportunity for a free drink. I'm not going to cry in my beer over it." But the truth was he had felt snubbed. Not because he thought he was God's gift but because she'd been standing alone and he'd taken pity on her. She was too beautiful to be hidden in a corner all night. And all he'd got for his trouble was a cold *no, thank you* and a chilly breeze as she left his presence in record time.

"Well, that's settled then." She ran a hand over the side of her hair, even though he couldn't see a strand out of place. It probably wouldn't dare be so impertinent. "Now if you'll excuse me, I have more important things to do."

"More important than impressing your main benefactor? Tsk, tsk."

He didn't know what made him say that. Sam didn't usually resort to throwing his weight around. Something about Angela Beck rubbed him the wrong way. It was as though she'd sized him up at first glance and found him wanting. And that grated, especially since he was already in a foul mood. He'd been late when he prided himself on punctuality. His last meeting with the engineers for the biogas facility had gone well over the time expected and had had less than satisfactory results.

Sam was used to being ahead of the curve, not behind it.

He was set to apologize when she stood, placing her palms flat on the table. "This is about helping abused women, not stroking your ego. Your mother understands that. Perhaps you can suggest an alternative proxy for the board position as clearly you do not care about the cause."

Well, well. She had fire, he'd give her that. And it was all wrapped in a package that momentarily took his breath now that he could see her from head to…well, mid thigh, anyway. She had curves under the neat and tidy librarian clothes—straight black skirt and plain buttoned-down blouse. But she had him to rights and he knew it. And they both knew that Molly had stipulated a Diamond family member sit on the board and not the other way around. He was the only other Diamond in Cadence Creek. There *was* no one else.

He stood slowly, reached for his hat and put it back on his head. "Ma'am."

He was nearly to the door when he heard her sigh. "Mr. Diamond?"

He paused, his hand on the door handle. He turned his head to look at her and realized she'd taken off her glasses again. Her eyes really were stunning. And he shouldn't be noticing.

"Your mother didn't believe in simply throwing money at a problem," Angela said quietly. "She believed in being part of the solution. I find it strange she'd ask you to take her place if she didn't think you'd hold up that end of the bargain."

It wasn't that he didn't care, or that Butterfly House wasn't a good cause. He just had too much on his plate. Angela Beck was being far too smart. She'd worded her last statement in just the right way to flatter and to issue a finely veiled challenge at the same time.

A challenge he wasn't up to accepting. The foundation had its land, had its house free and clear. That would have to be enough.

"Good day, Ms. Beck," he replied, and walked out, shutting the door behind him.

CHAPTER TWO

SAM pulled into the yard and killed the engine, resting his hands on the steering wheel. He hadn't been going to come. He had planned simply to leave well enough alone, go home to Diamondback, grab something to eat and collapse in bed so he'd be on his game for his daybreak wake-up call. Instead he'd found himself turning off the main road and driving through Cadence Creek, putting on his signal light and turning into the Butterfly House driveway. Angela Beck's last words bothered him more than he cared to admit, and he couldn't escape the need to make things right. He didn't necessarily want to apologize. He just wanted to explain why he'd acted the way he had today.

Angela was right. His mother *was* counting on him to step in now that she couldn't. He was a Diamond, and family was everything. He'd learned that at a young age, and it had been reinforced daily as he grew up alongside his cousin, Ty. Blood stuck together—no matter what Ty insisted these days.

The ranch wasn't the same with him gone, and Sam wished both Ty and Virgil would mend fences.

Sam was only doing this for Molly—Lord knew she'd sacrificed enough over the years for the Diamond men. It didn't sit well that he was probably going to let her down, too. So when Angela had accused him of just that, it had smarted more than he wanted to admit. He hadn't exactly acted like a gentleman by walking away. So now he'd just smooth things over and ease his conscience.

Resolved, he hopped out of the truck and shut the door. The rambling yellow Victorian house was full of add-on rooms, giving it a boxy, unsymmetrical appearance. It had once been in its glory but now the gingerbread trim beneath the eaves was dull and the paint was chipping. The front porch sagged as he took the first step. This was what the Diamond money had paid for? This falling-down monstrosity was going to be a progressive women's shelter? He frowned, then jumped as a train whistle sounded to the west, followed by the faint rumble of the cars on tracks. What a dump! And on the fringes of town. What had his mother been thinking, endorsing such a place?

He knocked on the door. It would be better if he just explained and left. He'd find the right time to deal with his mother. If he bided his time, she might even be back on the board within a month or two.

The door opened a crack. "Mr. Diamond?"

Ms. Beck's voice came through the crack, clearly surprised at seeing him standing on the ramshackle verandah. "Sam," he corrected, angling his neck to peer through the thin gap between door and frame.

"Sorry. If I open it further, Morris will get out. Again."

Morris? Sam sighed. Who on earth was Morris? *Give me strength*, he thought. He was starting to think that growing a conscience had been a big mistake. But he was here now. Might as well press on and then put it behind him. He had far bigger things to worry about when he got home. Like how to save the family that was falling apart.

"May I come in, then? I'll shut the door behind me."

Indecision twisted her face. She didn't want him inside Butterfly House. He knew it as sure as he knew he was breathing. What he didn't know was why. Maybe he'd been a little heavy-handed this afternoon, but nothing that should keep the door barred against him.

"I only want five minutes of your time," he said. "I don't like how we left things this afternoon."

She opened the door and he stepped inside, only to find it quickly shut again.

There was barely room to move around in the foyer. Plastic bags were scattered everywhere, along with cans of paint in various shades, the colors announced by dots on the silver lids. He side-stepped around them and pressed against the wall to allow Angela to move past and ahead of him. When she did, the panels of his sport coat brushed against her blouse. Something slid through him, something dark and familiar that came as a surprise. Angela sucked in a breath, clearly wanting to keep from touching him in any way, her eyes wide with alarm.

Just as well. She was pretty tightly wound and he preferred his women to be a little more easy-going. Angela Beck was the kind of woman who was work, and he had enough of that to last him a lifetime.

"I just got home a while ago," she said, leading the way into the kitchen. "Excuse the mess."

"I dropped in uninvited. No need to apologize." He walked around boxes stacked with linens and came to stand in the middle of the room.

"I was just having something to eat. Can I get you anything?"

He looked down at the concoction in cardboard she held in her hand. It appeared to be some sort of chicken and rice in a brownish sauce. "Not if it looks like that," he replied.

She performed a perfect shoulder shrug and said, "Suit yourself." She took another bite, but then got a strange look on her face and put the meal down on the counter. He wondered if she was going to ask him to sit down as the silence wound out awkwardly.

"So this is the house," he said casually, trying to put things on an even keel. He looked around the kitchen and then ignored his customary good manners and took a seat at the table, hoping she'd follow his lead and they could stop standing in the middle of the room. Small talk. He could manage a few minutes of that, couldn't he?

"It is."

"And how many residents will you have?"

"We split up the master bedroom and added a bathroom. At full capacity, we'll have five women and myself." She remained stubbornly standing, which made him feel even more like an unwanted guest she'd rather be rid of.

He nodded, wondering where to go next. Five tenants weren't many, but the shelter was only meant to be temporary—for as little as two months with a maximum of a year's occupancy. It would mean that a lot of abused women could find help in the run of a year. She was doing a good thing. He just didn't fit into the picture.

"Begging your pardon," she asked, "but why are you here...Sam?"

"Are you always this abrasive?"

Her mouth dropped open and she stared at him. "Are you always this blunt?"

"Yes," he replied without missing a beat. "What's

the point in dancing around anything? I tell it like it is. Makes it much easier to deal with issues."

Her mouth twisted. "In answer to your question, no," she admitted. "I'm usually not."

"Should I be flattered?" He couldn't resist asking. Flapping the seemingly unflappable Ms. Beck was an intriguing pastime.

"Hardly. You seem to bring out my worst."

Sam couldn't help it, he laughed. A low, dry chuckle built in his chest and the sound changed the air in the room, made it warmer. He looked up at her, watched as her gaze softened and her lips turned up the slightest bit in a reluctant smile. Desire, the same feeling he'd had as they'd brushed by each other in the foyer, gave a sharp kick. Angela Beck was an attractive woman. But when she became approachable, she was dangerous. The last thing he needed was to be tangled up in something messy and complicated. He'd been there and done that and it wasn't fun.

"Careful," he warned her. "You might smile."

"It's been known to happen. Once or twice. I'll try to restrain myself."

He was starting to appreciate her acid tongue, too. It spoke of a quick mind.

"Look," he said a little more easily, "I didn't feel right about how I spoke to you this afternoon. I have nothing against you personally, or your project. It's simply a case of hours in a day and only so much of me to go around, and I was in a bad mood when I arrived at the meeting. I meant what I said," he continued, "but I didn't put it in a very nice way."

"You're stepping back from the board then?"

She didn't have to sound so hopeful about it. He frowned. "I didn't say that. I just mean that the Diamond family assistance will be more of a behind-the-scenes kind of thing."

He didn't like the way her lips pursed. She should be glad he was still amenable to signing the checks.

"Your mother..."

"I know," he replied, cutting her off and growing impatient with the constant reminder of his mother's wishes. He stood up and faced Angela, wondering how it was possible that she could be getting under his skin so easily—again. "But I'm not my mother. My mother is in her sixties, her family is grown and she was looking for a cause to champion, something to fill her day with purpose. I don't need such a thing. Surely you can see how our time demands are completely different? My being here is entirely because it means something to her. But don't ask for more than that. I don't have it to give."

"That's what most people say," she responded. "I thank you for wanting to mend fences, but you're really just repeating yourself, Mr. Diamond. Butterfly House is low on your list of priorities."

Why did she have to make it sound like a character flaw? Sam bit his tongue, but she was making it hard with her holier-than-thou stance.

"What if I asked you to come out to the ranch tomorrow? Spend the day, take a tour?"

"I can't afford to take a day away from here!" Her lips dropped open in dismay. "There's too much to be done!"

He sat back, pleased that she'd taken the bait. "Exactly my point."

"It's hardly the same," she argued, wrapping her arms around her middle, the movement closing herself off from him even further. "You can hardly compare the Diamondback Ranch with this place. The differences are laughable."

She thought the Diamondback ranch was a joke? His blood heated. "Why do you disapprove of me so much?"

"Please," she said, contempt clear in her tone. "I've worked with people a long time. I know your type."

He bristled. His *type*? What exactly was his type? He didn't profess to be perfect but all he tried to do was put in an honest day's work. He knew he had a bit of a reputation for being single-minded, but what was so wrong with that? He knew what he wanted, and he went after it. There was something else in her tone, the same negative inflection she'd used the night of the benefit. It grated that she made that sort of snap judgment without even getting to know him at all. She had no idea of the pressure he was under these days.

"Really. And you came to this judgment somewhere between me offering you a drink at the fundraiser and walking through the door at the meeting today?"

She looked slightly uncomfortable and he noticed her fingers picked at the fabric in her skirt. "Among other sources."

"Ah, I see. And these other sources would be?"

She lifted her gaze and something sparked in her eyes. "You are not going to turn this on me, Mr. Diamond."

"Oh, don't worry, Ms. Beck." He put particular emphasis on the *Ms.*, hoping to get a rise out of her. Snap judgments that she wouldn't even qualify annoyed him. He was gratified to see her nostrils flare the slightest bit. "Because I know your type, too, but I'm too much of a gentleman to elaborate."

"A gentleman!" she exclaimed. Sparks flashed in her eyes. "From what I hear, you're far from a gentleman."

Sam wasn't in the mood to defend his character as well as today's actions. He had never, not once, been dishonest with a woman. He wondered where she'd gotten her information from and if it had anything to do with Amy Wilson? Dating her had been a mistake and he'd done her a favor by setting her free. But Amy hadn't seen it that way and had felt compelled to complain all over town. Most people knew to take it for what it was—sour grapes and hurt feelings. But Angela was new here and Amy could be very persuasive.

He had come here to apologize only to have his good intentions thrown back in his face and his character maligned. His temper flared. "Before you say anything more, think very carefully," he cautioned. "I'm sure you don't want to lose Diamond funding. If I recall, even with the house bought and paid for, there are operating expenses to consider. Not to mention your salary."

He saw her face go pale and felt his insides shrivel. Dammit. They were right back where they'd started despite all his resolve to smooth out the wrinkles. It was beneath him to threaten funding and yet he couldn't bring himself to back down. He'd look even more foolish. He should have put a stop to Amy's gossip ages ago, but he'd felt bad after the breakup, knowing he'd hurt her without intending to.

Now he'd gone and acted like a bully. He sighed and wiped a hand over his face, uttering a low curse. "What is it about you that brings out the worst in me?"

"The truth?" she replied acidly.

Angela's stomach seemed to drop to her feet as the words slid from her lips. She couldn't take them back and they echoed through the kitchen. He had just confirmed her opinion. Everything Amy had said about him really was true. He was caught up in himself and no one else, wasn't he? She really should learn to shut her mouth. More than anything else, the need to smooth the waters rather than make waves was the one thing she'd never quite eradicated from her own life.

Her head said to placate him because his funds were crucial to the project. But her pride—and her heart—wanted to tell him exactly what she thought. What sort of example would she set if she allowed him to threaten her job, the very existence of the project? The whole purpose of the shelter was to help women stand on their own two feet, to be strong. How could she allow herself to be weak? She certainly couldn't give in to the urge to back down every time she faced a challenge.

While she was contemplating her response, Morris chose that moment to strut through the kitchen. Lord of the house, master and protector, the orange-and-cream-colored cat stopped and regarded Sam with a judgmental eye.

"The infamous Morris?" Sam asked.

"I should have called him Houdini," Angela responded. "He's quite the escape artist." It was unusual for Morris to come out when strangers were around, and she watched as he made his way over to Sam. Maybe she'd judged Sam too harshly before. You could tell a lot about a man by watching him with animals.

Morris went directly to Sam, surprising her, and he sniffed at Sam's jeans suspiciously. Sam looked at Angela helplessly, shrugging his shoulders. Angela saw the fur on Morris's back stand up and his tail stiffen. She took a step forward, opening her mouth to warn Sam. But she was too late. Sam shouted and looked down at his leg, rubbing the denim just above the top of his boot.

Morris scooted away, but Angela knew exactly what had happened and wanted to sink through the floor. She hadn't thought this meeting could get any worse, but Morris had taken matters into his own…teeth.

"Your cat bit me!"

Heat rushed to her face as his words moved her to action. She scrambled after Morris and picked him up. Cursed animal, he snuggled into her arms sweet as honey. "He has a thing about strangers. Particularly men." She rushed to the half bath and locked Morris inside. "I think he was abused as a kitten," she continued, wondering if there was anything more she could do to make Sam Diamond more aggravated. "The vet said his tail was broken in three places, that's why it's crooked. But he really isn't a bad cat, he just has a protective streak. He…"

Her voice trailed off. Sam was staring at her as

though she was crazy. "I'll shut up now," she murmured.

"Really," Sam said drily, as if she'd stated the impossible.

Morris meowed in protest, the howl only barely muffled through the door.

"You're a real bleeding heart, aren't you, Ms. Beck?" He glowered at her. "Maybe I need to come up with a better sob story, eh? Maybe that'll get you off my back."

That did it. "Since when did helping others become a flaw, Diamond?" She took a step forward, feeling her temper get the better of her. "Maybe if you took your head out of your charmed, privileged life for two seconds you'd see someone other than yourself. And as far as Morris goes, maybe I am a bleeding heart because I can't stand to see another creature abused. And if he's a little leery of men, he has good reason. I consider him a fine judge of character!"

Sam's dark eyes flared. "A fine judge of..." He made a sound like air whistling out of a tube. Morris howled again. "You know nothing about me. Nothing."

"I know you're a big bully who thinks I'll dance to his tune because I need his money. But I won't pander to you like Charles Spring and the others on the board. You can threaten, you can take funding away. Go for it. Because I would rather that than me betray all Butterfly House stands for by letting myself be pushed around by the likes of you." She finished the speech out of breath.

"Without the funding, this place never opens."

"Don't be so sure." Several times today she'd allowed Sam Diamond to mess with her confidence. But she was done with that. She'd faced worse than Sam Diamond over the years and come through with flying colors. Besides, she had an ace in the hole. She knew Molly Diamond was dedicated to this project. Molly believed in it and in her.

"You think I haven't faced adversity before?" She pressed her hand to her collarbone, felt her heart pounding against her fingertips. "I'm stronger and more resourceful than you think. So go for it. Pull the funding."

She wasn't sure what made her dare him to do such a thing when they clearly pushed each other's buttons so completely and quickly. That had only happened to her once before when she'd been seventeen and so very vulnerable. She'd fallen for Steven in record time and found herself smack in the middle of a volatile relationship. Her mother had taken one look at Angela's face and said quietly, "Passion burns as hot as anger, dear." But that wasn't the kind of passion Angela ever wanted, and her parents certainly hadn't set a shining example for her to follow.

It took everything she had to stand toe-to-toe

with Sam Diamond now without cowering. And yet, as she looked into his handsome face, she somehow knew that she wasn't being entirely fair. She was making connections, assumptions without basis. All through her career she'd worked very hard to be objective. She'd had to be.

So Sam Diamond shouldn't be any different. But he was. And she admitted to herself that he had been from the moment he'd sauntered over and spoken to her in his slow, sexy voice at the benefit. Nerve endings had shimmered just at his nearness. He posed a different threat than physical fear. And that threat came from inside herself and her own weaknesses.

He hooked his thumbs into his pockets. "I'm not going to pull the funding. The Diamond family made a commitment, and we honor our commitments despite what some may think."

The tension in the room seemed to settle slightly, no longer at a fever pitch amplified by sharp words.

"I appreciate that."

He took a step closer and her heart started a different sort of thrumming. Earlier she'd taken great care to make sure she didn't touch him as they passed in the crowded hallway. She stood her ground. She didn't want him to know she was afraid. Goodness, she was a strong, capable, resourceful woman. It was ridiculous that one person could make her forget all of that just by breathing.

She tried to remember what it was that Amy had said. That Sam Diamond took what he wanted until he was done and then he tossed it away like yesterday's garbage. Amy's words were completely opposite from Sam's pledge, so which should she believe?

"You're tired," he noted, and to her shock he lifted his hand and ran his thumb along the top of her cheekbone. She knew there were dark circles beneath her eyes. Makeup had concealed it for most of the day, but it was growing late and as the makeup faded, her fatigue came to the surface.

But more than that—he was touching her. She flinched slightly at the presumptuous yet gentle touch, but he didn't seem to notice. His thumb was large, strong and just a little rough. She was tempted to lean in to the strength of his hand for just a minute, but she held her face perfectly still instead as her insides quivered with a blend of attraction and fear. "I've been putting in long days," she breathed. "There's a lot to do."

"I won't keep you, then," he replied, dropping his hand. She missed the warmth of his thumb and took a step backward, shocked at her response. No one ever touched her. Ever. And certainly not in such an intimate way.

"I'm sorry about Morris. He's a very naughty cat. Did he get you very badly?"

And then it happened. Angela saw the barest hint

of a smile touch his lips. Not the smooth, charming grin from this afternoon. A conspiratorial upturning of his lips that Angela couldn't resist. It sneaked past all her misgivings and lit something inside her. She found herself smiling in return and chuckling. He joined in, the warm sound filling the kitchen.

Angela sighed as the laughter faded, looked over at Sam's face, now holding a spot of devilishness that made her understand why the women of this town all swooned in his presence.

"I'll live," he said, the earlier hostility gone. "It was more of a surprise, really." He lifted an eyebrow. "Just as well I have a tough skin. Maybe he smelled our dog or something. Buster has a way of putting cats on edge."

Was he teasing her now? The idea made an unfamiliar warmth curl through her. She had to admit, knowing he was a pet owner added to his appeal. She had a momentary image of Sam on a huge horse with a dog following at their heels....

Dangerous. And trouble. At the very least, Amy had that part right.

"Don't take it personally," she offered weakly. "It's not you..."

"If you say so."

"I couldn't just leave him," she continued, not knowing why it was important that Sam understand about her cat but feeling compelled just the same.

Another meow sounded behind the door. "He was hurt, and just a baby."

Sam's face was inscrutable. "Do I strike you as the kind of man who kicks puppies, Ms. Beck?"

Did he? Lord, no. He might use charm as a weapon, and he might have a ruthless streak—that single-mindedness he'd mentioned—but she found it hard to believe he'd be deliberately cruel. There was something about the way he'd touched her face…

She shook her head, not quite trusting her judgment.

"Well, that's something, then."

He turned to walk down the hall, back toward the front door, around the bags of home-renovation supplies and paint and everything else that would take up all her waking moments for the next several days. Perhaps weeks.

Maybe she could sweet-talk someone local into donating their time. School would be out for summer soon. Maybe a couple of students at loose ends… There was so much to do before the open house. The logistics of organizing that alone were taking up so much time and energy, and she'd already drafted the press release and sent it out.…

The press release. The media was going to expect to see Molly at that, too. New nerves tangled as she thought of dealing with the press alone. She looked up at Sam. Getting more from him would be like getting blood from a stone. She'd figure something out. She had a little bit of time.

"I'd better let you get back to your dinner," he said, putting his hand on the doorknob.

Her dinner. The tasteless glazed chicken that she'd popped in the microwave in lieu of a real meal.

"I trust that I'll see you next month at the board meeting, then?"

His hat shadowed his eyes in the dim light of the foyer, so when he nodded briefly Angela couldn't read his expression. Something between them hesitated, seemed to keep him from opening the door, made it feel that there was more to her question than she'd voiced—and more to his answer.

When she finally thought he must be able to hear her heart beating through her chest, he opened the door. Angela let out a deep sigh of relief, until he turned and tipped his finger to his hat in farewell.

A gentleman.

She shut the door behind him. Perhaps. But not like any gentleman she'd ever known. And maybe that was the problem.

CHAPTER THREE

SHE'D been kidding herself.

Exhausted, Angela sank down on the lopsided front step and put her head in her hands. For ten days she'd worked her tail off, and there was still so much to do her head was spinning. Having to do the renovations herself meant no time for working on the embellishments, the little special touches she'd had in mind. The basement was littered with used paint cans and rollers, and she'd missed a stud trying to install a curtain rod and ended up having to do a substantial drywall repair in the yellow room. Yards of material gathered dust waiting to be sewn into curtains and duvet covers. Boxes of supplies were still taped up, needing to be unpacked. The carpet was torn up in the living room but the local flooring business had postponed installation of the new hardwood until tomorrow. The place was a mess.

The open house was only four days away. She needed Molly's help. Molly had been on board to look after feeding the crew from the youth center on Saturday. She was also supposed to be a spokesperson to the media so Angela could stay in the background, where she liked it. Angela had been so annoyed by Sam's attitude that she'd squared her shoulders and determined she'd show him and do it all herself.

But she'd been wrong. She needed help. And she needed *his* help if Molly wasn't able. It wasn't just about a pair of spare hands. The press release had gone out before that horrible board meeting and the local angle had been playing up Diamond involvement. To go ahead with the day and have the Diamonds conspicuously absent…to stand in front of a camera and have her picture taken, her words put into print…

Her stomach tied up in knots just thinking about it. This wasn't about her, it was about *them*—the women the foundation would help. The last thing she needed was anyone digging around in her past. She closed her eyes. It was truly a bad state if she was relying on the likes of Sam Diamond to be her ally!

She wiped her hands on her overalls, resigned. It came back to the same thing every time, no matter how much she didn't want to admit it.

She needed Sam Diamond's help.

* * *

She found him coming down a beaten track on horseback, sitting a trot effortlessly while a golden retriever loped along behind. Growing up in the city she hadn't really believed that cowboys and ranchers, like those in storybooks and movies, really existed. But they did. The Diamondback Ranch sprawled over the foothills, dotted with red-and-white cattle. The house was a huge log-type mansion that reeked of money and Western tradition at once. Just beyond a gigantic barn was a paddock where half a dozen gleaming horses snoozed in the warmth of the summer sun. And Sam Diamond was getting closer by the second, all six foot plus of him in his own über-masculine element.

She'd never felt so out of place in her life, and she'd been in some pretty uncomfortable spots over the years.

"Well, well. Must be important to tear yourself away from Butterfly House on such a gorgeous day."

She had to squint against the sun to look up at him. "You manage to compliment the weather and antagonize me all in the same sentence," she said. She forced a small smile. "And I might get mad, except for the fact that you're right. It is important."

He'd slowed to a walk but she still had to hustle to keep up with him.

"And it has to do with me...why?"

With a slight shift of the reins, horse and rider

came to a stop. The dog, sensing home, bounded off in the direction of the house. Angela held her breath as Sam turned in the saddle and looked directly at her. On horseback he was an imposing figure, and he had a direct way of looking at a person that was intimidating. She wasn't comfortable being one hundred percent of his focus, but she made herself meet his gaze. He looked far too good for comfort in his jeans, boots and dark Stetson, and she took her sunglasses out of her hair and put them on, shading her eyes.

The horse Sam rode was big and black, and the way he tossed his head made his bridle hardware jingle. He was exactly the kind of mount she'd expect Sam Diamond to ride—big and bossy and used to having his way. But Angela refused to be intimidated.

When she didn't answer, he grinned. "Let's try that again, shall we? Good mornin', Ms. Beck. To what do I owe the pleasure?"

There was a mocking note to his words and Angela felt his gaze drop over her clothing and back up again. She'd considered changing out of her paint-streaked overalls and sneakers but decided not to. She felt safer in the shapeless garment rather than her work clothes that skimmed her figure more closely. Besides, the scale of work that had to be done was enormous. Fixing herself up would have taken valuable time she couldn't afford to lose.

"I need your help."

There, she'd said it, and it only hurt a little. Mostly in her pride.

"My help? My, my. That must have been hard to say."

"Yes. I mean no. You see…I had counted on your mother's help and without it I've fallen behind. I know it couldn't be helped," she rushed to add. "I don't blame Molly. She belongs with your father, of course. I've tried for the last week and a half to keep pace on my own, but we've got a press opportunity happening this Saturday and I'm not ready."

"As you can see, I've got my hands full here."

"Surely you can spare some time? I've been doing the renovations myself but there are some things I'm just not equipped to do. The front step is a hazard and the furniture needs to be moved into the living room before Saturday and somehow I have to have refreshments on hand for a dozen teenagers who will be at the house. Not to mention the press."

She was quite breathless at the end and felt a blush infuse her cheeks as Sam merely raised one eyebrow until it disappeared from view beneath his hat.

"Come to the house. I'll write you a check and you can hire some help for a few days."

Her blood began to simmer. For most people she would have said *put your money where your mouth is*. But for Sam, writing a check was an easy way to rid himself of the inconvenience of her and of Butterfly House. Her annoyance temporarily overrode her personal discomfort.

"You don't understand. This isn't just about slapping on some paint. It's about perception."

"Perception?"

"Yes, perception." She sighed. "It's not even so much the renovations. When you replaced Molly on the board, the press releases had already been sent and the arrangements made. You're the foundation's biggest sponsor, Sam. And everyone expects to see a Diamond presence this weekend. If there's no one there…"

"If it's perception you're worried about, I'm not sure I'm the image you want to present to the public. You'll do fine without me."

He laughed, but Angela wasn't amused. This project was about more than helping women reclaim their lives. It was about changing attitudes. And Sam Diamond, with his money and swagger, was the perfect test case. If she could bring him around, she figured she could accomplish just about anything.

"I won't say no to the check because the foundation needs it. But we need more than that, too. We need a showing of support. We need the backing of the community. I don't like it any more than you do. I wish I didn't need your help. But I sat on the step this morning trying to figure out how I was going to manage it all and I kept coming up blank."

"Maybe I can spare a man for a day or two, but that's all. Now, if you'll excuse me."

But that wasn't all. How easy was it for Sam to solve a problem by scrawling a dollar amount and washing his hands of it? "All I'm asking for is one day. One day for you to show up, be charming, give a visible show of support. As much as it pains me to admit it, the people of Cadence Creek follow your lead."

He rolled his eyes. "Here we go again. You don't give up, do you? Do you ever take no for an answer?"

She gritted her teeth. If he only knew how much she hated confrontation! She lifted her chin. "Do *you*?"

A magpie chattered, breaking the angry silence. "From the look of the house, it needs more than a slap of paint. It needs a demolition order. You'll never get it fixed by Saturday." Sam adjusted the reins as his horse danced, impatient at being forced to stand.

Angela got close enough that she had to tilt her head to look up at Sam. She wanted him to see what was at stake. It wasn't enough for him to sit atop his ivory tower of privilege—or his trusty steed—and bestow his beneficence. It was too easy. And the women she wanted to help hadn't had it easy. Their lives couldn't be fixed by a blank check.

"I have to. The house has been neglected, that's all. It just needs some TLC."

"Ms. Beck." He sighed, looking down at her from beneath his hat. "Do you want me to do everything for you?"

She felt her cheeks heat. "Of course not. But, for example, I was going to look after the painting and minor renovations while your mother lent a hand with some of the aesthetic needs—like window fashions, linens. On Saturday she was not only going to represent your family to the community and press, but she was in charge of all the refreshments. That's all fallen to me now. I do need to sleep sometime, Sam. And then there's the issue of what to say to people on Saturday when they ask about our biggest sponsor and their conspicuous absence."

"You tell them we're busy running a ranch. You tell them we're occupied with adding a new green facility to our operation. Or that we're busy employing a number of the town residents. All true, by the way."

"Have you heard of volunteering, Mr. Diamond?"

His dark eyes widened as his brows went up. "I beg your pardon?"

"Volunteering—offering one's time with no expectation of reimbursement."

"I know what volunteering is," he replied, impatience saturating each word.

"Millions of people volunteer every day and still manage to work their day jobs. Most of them also have families of their own—and you don't have a wife or children that I can see. You can spare Butterfly House the cash, but can you spare it the time?"

Angela swallowed, took a breath, and stepped forward, grabbing the reins of his horse with far more confidence than she felt. She stood in front of the stallion's withers, her body only inches away from Sam's denim-clad leg as it lengthened into the stirrup. "What are you so afraid of, Sam?"

He slid out of the saddle and snatched the reins from her hands, his movements impatient. "You can save the holier-than-thou routine. I've made up my mind."

She could sense success slipping away from her and frustration bubbled. "You go to great lengths to avoid personal involvement. Why is that? Maybe it's true what they say about you."

"And what's that?" He stood before her, all long legs and broad chest. She felt incredibly small and awkward next to his physicality, dumpy in her overalls next to his worn jeans and cotton shirt that seemed to hug his shoulders and chest. She felt a little bit awed, too, and it irritated her that she should be so susceptible to that because, despite the fact he was a pain in the behind, Sam Diamond was also drop-dead sexy. The sad thing was she was nearly thirty years old and had no idea what to do with these feelings. She'd gotten very good at presenting a certain image, but inside she knew the truth. She had no idea how to be close to anyone.

"Never mind." She turned away, hating that he was able to provoke her without even trying.

He reached out and grabbed her wrist. "Not so fast. I think you'd better tell me."

Her heart seemed to freeze as her breath caught for one horrible, chilling moment. Then, very carefully and deliberately, she reached down and removed his fingers from her wrist and stepped back. She wasn't sure which emotion was taking over at the moment—anger or fear. But either one was enough to make the words that had been sitting on her tongue come out in a rush.

"That you're a cold-hearted…" She couldn't bring herself to say the word. She kept her gaze glued to his face for several seconds.

Finally the hard angle of his jaw bone softened a touch and he said quietly, "Where'd you hear that? Let me guess, Amy Wilson?"

She had, and her lack of response confirmed it.

"You shouldn't judge someone by what you hear."

"I don't." At his skeptical expression, she sniffed. "I don't," she insisted. "I form my own opinions. I deal with people all the time, you know. And I judge people by what I see them do." And right now he wasn't scoring many points. Her wrist still smarted from the strength of his fingers circling the soft flesh. She touched the spot with her fingers.

His gaze caught the movement and then lifted to meet hers. There was contrition there, she realized. He hadn't really hurt her; he'd merely reached out to keep her from running away. It was her reaction that was out of proportion and she suspected they both knew it. Awkward silence stretched out as heat rose once again in her cheeks.

"And so you've judged me." The horse got tired of standing and jerked his head, pulling on the reins. Sam tightened his grip, uttered a few soothing words as he gave the glistening neck a pat. "I suppose you won't believe me if I say I'm sorry about that." He nodded at her clasped hands.

It was a backward apology, and did nothing to change the situation. That was what she had to remember. "Sam, you give from your pocketbook if it means you don't have to get involved. I just haven't figured out why. Is the ugliness of real life too much for you?" She kissed her last hope of success goodbye, knowing she was crossing a line but needing to say it anyway. How many times over the years had people turned a blind eye to someone in trouble? How many people had avoided the nasty side of life because it made them uncomfortable? How many people had known what was happening in front of their faces and hadn't had the courage to make the call? Angela's life might have been very different. It was the only thing that kept her moving forward in spite of her own fears.

"That's ridiculous." He turned his back and started leading his horse across the barnyard.

"Then prove it. Try giving of yourself." She went after him, desperately wanting to get through. "These women have been through it all, Sam. They've been beaten, degraded, raped…" She swallowed. "By the men who professed to love them. Despite it all, they got out. They sought help, often leaving everything they owned behind. This house will help bridge the gap between overcoming an old life and building a new, shiny one. What in your life is more important than that?"

He didn't answer. But she sensed he was weakening, and she softened her voice. "All I'm asking for is a few hours here and there. You have a gorgeous house, food on the table, a purpose. I just want to give these women the same chance. If you show the people of Cadence Creek that you support these women, doors will open. They'll have a chance to be a part of something. People look to you to lead. Lead now, Sam. For something really important."

She took a step back, uncomfortable with how impassioned her voice had become. For a few seconds there was nothing but the sounds of the wind in the grass and the songbirds in the bushes.

"You realize how busy this ranch is, right? And that I'm going it alone now that Dad's sick?"

"But you have a foreman, and hands. Surely they can spare you for a few hours?"

"You're forgetting one important detail."

"I am?"

"If I help you, we're going to be seeing more of each other." He made it sound like a prison sentence. "And I don't mean to be rude, but we're kind of like oil and water."

She felt her vanity take a hit before locking it away. Her personal feelings weren't important here. It shouldn't matter if Sam liked her or not. She only needed his support.

"Don't worry. There's lots of house to go around. We hardly have to see each other. I can stand it if you can." Besides, there were lines she didn't cross, ever, and it was a big leap from noticing the fit of a man's jeans to personal involvement. They rubbed each other the wrong way. Then she remembered how he'd brushed by her the other night and how her body had suddenly become attuned to his. The real trouble was in the few moments where they had rubbed each other exactly the right way. At least on Saturday there would be tons of other people around and she'd be too busy keeping the kids busy and the food on the go to worry about Sam.

They were at the fence gate now and there wasn't much left to say. He threw the reins up over the saddle horn and mounted, settling into the saddle with a creak of leather. "I'm not afraid," he said. "Two hours. I'll give you two hours Saturday afternoon to talk to whatever press you've lined up. Just keep your social-worker analysis to yourself, okay? I'm not interested. Save it for your clients."

"Scouts' honor," she replied, lifting two fingers to her brow. She couldn't help the smile that curved her lips. It wasn't all she'd asked for, but more than she'd dare hoped and she counted it as a significant victory. Perhaps she'd be spared the public face after all.

He shook his head and gave the horse a nudge. As they were walking away he twisted in the saddle, looking back at her. "I'll send over a check. I'd advise you to cash it before I change my mind and stop payment on it. Maybe you can cater your food for Saturday with it."

He showed her his back again and they took off at a trot, stirring up dust.

* * *

Sam looked up from his desk and realized it was nearly dark outside. That meant… He checked his watch. It was going on ten o'clock. He'd been at it longer than he realized. But he wanted to start the construction on the new project before the end of summer, marking a new era for Diamondback. As he got older the more he realized he was caretaker not only of the Diamondback name but the land. The environmentally friendly initiatives were exciting, and he loved the idea of reducing Diamondback's footprint. But his father's stubborn refusal to sign off on the contracts was stressing him out.

He sighed, rubbed a hand over his face. It grated on his nerves, having the responsibility of the ranch without also having the authority to make the changes he wanted. And with Virgil's health so precarious, he was doing some fancy footwork these days trying to get his way without upsetting the proverbial apple cart. Between his father and the everyday running of the ranch, he hadn't been lying when he'd told Angela that he didn't have a moment to spare.

But then she'd had to go and challenge him and he'd been suckered in. It rankled that she knew how to push his buttons without really knowing him at all. He didn't think he was usually so transparent.

She'd looked exhausted. There was the annoying realization that she'd been right in just about everything. A Diamond family member *had* promised to appear and her assertion that Butterfly House would need community support was valid.

But for Sam it had been more than that. It had been the look in her eyes, the way all the color had leached from her cheeks in the split second he'd grasped her wrist within his fingers. The expression had been enough to give even his jaded heart a wrench. There was more to Angela than the prim and proper businesswoman he'd met at the board meeting. This was personal for her and he wanted to know why.

He scowled. It was none of his business. The last thing he needed was to get sucked into someone else's problems. If only his mother would agree to a hired nurse, she could go back to being Angela's right hand and cheerleader. He worried about Molly, taking on all of his father's care herself and refusing any help. With a sigh he closed his eyes. He was trying to hold everything together and not doing a great job of it.

A light knock sounded at the door and he turned in his chair. "Mom. You're still up?"

Molly Diamond came in, and Sam thought she looked older than she had a few short weeks ago. There were new lines around her eyes and mouth, and she'd lost weight. The light sweater she wore seemed to hang from her shoulders.

"I just got your father settled. You're up late."

"Just going over the latest information on the

biogas facility. I'm close to finally having the details nailed down. The sooner the better, we've had enough delays. I'm excited about it."

"Sam…" Molly's brow furrowed. "Right now those plans are more like building castles in the sand."

"Then help me convince him," he replied easily. "He won't listen to me. This will take Diamondback into the future."

"What sort of future? Who for, Sam?"

There it was again. The constant tone that said *when are you going to start a family?* Surely she realized it wasn't a simple snap of the fingers to find the right woman. There had to be love. Whoever he married was taking on not only him but Diamondback as well. He gritted his teeth. "Two different subjects, Mom. And right now this facility is the right thing."

Molly sighed. "It's a big undertaking. And your father sacrificed a lot to make Diamondback what it is. He's just…cautious. Please don't trouble him about it. Not now."

"It's the way of the future. And I've spent a lot of hours putting this together." Disappointment was clear in his voice.

"And it's taking its toll," she said, coming to the desk and pulling up a chair. The desk lamp cast a circle of cozy light and despite the recent troubles, Sam thought how lucky he was to have grown up here. It hadn't always been easy, and there'd been a good many arguments and slammed doors, especially in younger years.

But he'd never once questioned their love, never once felt insecure. He thought of Angela, standing in the farmyard in paint-smeared, shapeless overalls and dark glasses. He wondered what her upbringing had been like, thought about the women who would benefit from Butterfly House. Not everyone had had the advantages that he'd had.

"What's really on your mind, Sam?"

"Nothing, really. Just trying to keep up."

"You met Angela Beck," Molly said, leaning back against the cushion of the chair and crossing her legs. "She's a worker."

"A dog with a bone, more like it," he muttered. Molly laughed and it was good to hear the sound. Ever since she'd found his father on the floor of their bedroom after his stroke, there hadn't been much to laugh about.

"She's doing a good thing, Sam."

"I know. But you're much better at this kind of thing than I am. I belong out there." He lifted his chin, looking out the window. In the darkness, only the reflection from the lamp looked back at him. "We totally rub each other the wrong way. We can't occupy the same space without arguing. I have intentions of being nice, and I end up being an idiot."

To his surprise Molly laughed. "At least you acknowledge when you're an idiot," she answered, "which puts you a step ahead of most of the population."

"Mom, why don't you let me hire some help for you?" He leaned forward, resting his elbows on the desk. "Then you can still work on this project. It'll be good for you." Plus it would mean he wouldn't be pulled away from the farm, and he wouldn't have to come face-to-face with Angela's acute observations—never mind her smoky eyes and delicious curves. She'd tried to hide them in the overalls, but they were still there. He didn't like that he kept noticing. Didn't like that she seemed to be on his mind more often than not.

"Because I want to be with your father." Molly looked tired, but Sam noticed how her eyes warmed. "You'll understand someday, when you're married and you've been in love with that person for most of your life."

Sam sighed. "Mom, I'm thirty-seven. Don't count on it, okay? At this rate, Ty's your best chance for a grandkid."

Ty. Sam's cousin by blood but also his adoptive brother. Any child of his would be considered a grandchild. But Ty was barely on speaking terms with the family. Neither said it but they knew it was true. He hadn't even come home for Virgil's seventieth birthday.

"I'm not saying that, don't panic. I'm just saying

that I need to do this for Virgil. And that leaves Butterfly House up to you. It's not a long commitment. Once it's fixed up, the management of it will be in Angela's fine hands. A board meeting here and there is not too much to ask."

"You failed to mention the open house this weekend. She was here today, demanding I show up."

Molly put a hand to her head. "Oh, my word, I'd forgotten about that. I promised to help. We wrote the press releases together, before your dad…"

Her voice broke and Sam's heart gave a lurch. "It's okay. I told her I'd show up and do all the official handshaking. But, Mom, I can't go on doing this forever. I'm too busy. Maybe Dad will improve enough that you can step back in after a month or so," Sam suggested, shutting his folder.

"Maybe. But, Sam…"

He looked into Molly's dark eyes, eyes that reminded him of who he saw in the mirror. She was the strongest woman he knew, and he liked to think he'd inherited some of that strength.

"You've been brought up to believe that Diamondback is everything, but it's not, not really. Sometimes I think your Dad and I sheltered you too much, made it too easy on you. We wanted things to be better for you than they were for us starting out, but you've never really seen what it's like to be hurting, and struggling, and wondering if life will ever be good again."

"So this is for my own good?"

She chuckled. "You'll thank me one day, you'll see."

"Don't count on it." But he couldn't help the smile that curved his lips.

"I know you didn't sign up for this, Sam. But it would mean a lot to me if you could help out." Molly put her hands on the arms of the chair and boosted herself up. She gave a small stretch. "Well, I'm off to make a cup of tea before bed. Tomorrow's another day."

"I think I'll look in on Dad before I turn in."

"He was awake when I left. He lives for your updates, Sam. I know you're butting heads right now, but keep talking. He needs you. He needs to feel a part of this place."

Sam nodded, clicked off the light and followed his mother to the office door. They parted ways in the hall—Molly to the kitchen, Sam to the main level spare room, where his parents had slept ever since Virgil's stroke.

When he looked in, his father was asleep. Sam's heart gave a hitch. His larger-than-life father was reduced to a bed and a wheelchair. His words were muffled and unclear and he seemed so different from the giant who had slain boyhood dragons, from the man who had built this ranch, living for—and off—the land.

Now it was all up to Sam.

He could understand his father going crazy. He could even understand why Virgil was fighting so hard to remain in control. Because Sam couldn't imagine a day where he didn't wake up under a Diamondback sky and smell the Diamondback air. Why couldn't Virgil see they were fighting for the same thing?

CHAPTER FOUR

THE smell of paint hung in the air as Angela took another pin out of the curtain hem and carefully kept her foot on the pedal of the sewing machine. She'd planned simple curtains, tab-style that would thread through the pretty café rods she'd bought. Maybe it was the fabric that was causing the trouble, or maybe it was the fact that she'd been up and working for nearly twelve hours. Either way, she'd ripped out two seams already, and then indulged in an uncharacteristic spate of cursing when the bobbin thread tangled on the bottom.

She reversed, finished the seam, cut the threads and closed her eyes. There was still so much to do before Saturday. She was never going to make it this way.

"Is it safe to come in?"

She started in her chair as the deep voice echoed down the hall. "Sam?"

"None other." The screen door thumped into the frame and she pressed a hand to her pounding chest. She shouldn't be so jumpy, but it was an automatic reaction she'd been conditioned to years ago.

She hastily folded the fabric and put it on the kitchen table with the rest of the sewing bits. What on earth was he doing here? She hadn't expected to see him until Saturday afternoon.

His boots thumped on the wood floor and suddenly there he was, larger than life, in his customary jeans and boots but he'd traded his button-down shirt for a black T-shirt. The way the cotton stretched across his chest made her want to rest her hands against the surface to see if it was indeed as hard as it looked.

"What in the world?" His eyes widened as he took in the sight of the table.

She followed the path of his gaze. Not a glimpse of wood table was visible beneath the strewn-out cloth, pins and thread. More fabric hung over the back of one of the chairs and Morris batted a scrap along the floor, too entranced with the way it slithered over the tile to worry about Sam's presence.

"I'm not a neat seamstress," she remarked.

"I hope you have something else for me to do," he said, folding his arms. "Though I've been known to pick up a needle and thread before."

Angela swallowed. She tried to picture him in a chair, a tiny needle in his strong, wide hands, and it wouldn't gel. Sam was more untamed than that.

She looked up at his glittering eyes and decided *untamed* was a good word indeed. There was a restless energy about him that made her uneasy. Especially when what she needed from him was reliability.

He shrugged. "Of course, I'm usually stitching together hide and not dainties."

She would hardly call the blue damask *dainties*, but she didn't bother correcting him as now her mind was full of the image of him doctoring horses and cows. He was stubborn as a mule—she could see that plain as day. But she couldn't shake the idea that he'd treat his animals with capable and gentle hands.

Oh, dear. It wasn't a good idea to think of Sam Diamond in those terms. He was already looking a little too attractive.

"Do?"

"Yes, do. You didn't finish everything on your list, did you?"

Gracious, no. There was still lots to be done, but his sudden presence threw her utterly off balance. "I wasn't expecting you," she stammered.

"I thought you could use some help before the big day."

She kept her mouth shut for once, biting down on her lip and feeling a bit bad for all the nasty thoughts she'd had about him. She scrambled to come up with something he could do on the spur of the moment.

"Of course I can use the help. Um…I'm not exactly sure where to start."

"I brought some tools and supplies in the truck," he suggested, resting his weight on one hip. "You mentioned the other day that the porch steps and floor needed some work. Maybe I could tighten them up, replace a few boards. I don't think anything's rotted, but I won't know until I have a good look. In any case, you can't paint until it's repaired."

"That'd be fine," she replied, relieved he'd thought ahead and she wouldn't have to show him anything. It also meant he'd paid attention and given it some thought. It was what she'd wanted, right? For him to notice that Butterfly House needed help? So why was getting what she wanted making her so flustered?

"It'll give me a chance to clean up in here. I finished painting the blue room today. Your mother helped me pick out the fabric. That's what I'm sewing…"

"My mother and I have different skill sets."

She smiled, trying to imagine Sam debating the benefits of certain colors and fabrics or chatting about recipes. The image didn't fit. But visualizing him using his hands was something entirely different. For all his untamed energy and irritating ways, Angela was beginning to see that Sam was the kind of man who formed foundations. He shored up the weak spots and made them strong— at Diamondback and now here. She didn't want to be relieved at passing off even just a little of the responsibility, but she was, just the same.

"I'm happy to have your skills, since I'm not adept at construction. Some light carpentry work would be wonderful, Sam, thank you."

The words were friendly and for a moment neither of them said anything. Friendliness was a new vibe between them and Angela didn't quite know what to do with it. But wasn't it better than being at each other's throats all the time? If they could make peace, maybe this tight feeling in her chest that happened every time he was around would disappear.

"If I need anything I'll give a shout."

"I'll be here."

He treated her to one long, last look before turning on his heel. He was out of sight when he called out.

"Oh, and Angela? Be careful. You smiled just now. You might want to get that checked."

She balled her fingers into fists as the door shut behind him. Oh, he was impossible! Just when she thought they were coming to some common ground, he had to provoke her again. And yet there'd been a teasing note in his voice that made warmth seep into her. It was foreign, but it wasn't an unwelcome feeling.

She folded the finished panel and yanked out the second, all pinned and ready for stitching. At least he was out there and she was in here and she didn't have to look into his sexy, teasing face!

But the sound of the hammer could be heard over the hum of the machine, and Angela's brows knit together. Sam Diamond was not going to be an easy man to ignore.

He was still working on the porch when she finished pressing the last completed panel. Carefully she laid the curtains over the ironing board so they wouldn't wrinkle and tidied up her sewing mess. Twilight was starting to fall and he'd soon have to quit as he lost the light. Angela took a breath, considered, and then went to the fridge for the jug of lemonade she'd mixed up earlier. She poured two glasses and started for the front door. Whatever her misgivings where Sam was concerned, it would be nice if at Saturday's event they appeared as a team rather than on opposing sides. In hindsight, the incident earlier in the week had been pure overreaction on her part. Sam had made the first step coming here today. Now it was her turn.

She opened the screen door with a flick of her finger and a nudge of her hip. Sam looked up and for a moment Angela's heart seemed to hesitate as their gazes locked. There was a gleam of sweat on his forehead and as he stood, he hooked his hammer into his tool belt, a thoroughly masculine move that sent her heart rate fluttering.

Oh, my.

She'd never been particularly susceptible to the rugged workingman type before, but Sam was in a class of his own. And when he smiled and asked, "Is that for me?" the only thing she could do was extend her hand and give him the glass, careful not to let their fingers touch.

She held her own lemonade in her hand, forgotten, as he took two big swallows, tipping his head back so that she could see the movement in his throat. Her tongue snuck out to wet her lips. She'd bet any money the skin on his neck was salty and warm from his hard work.

He lowered the glass and Angela snapped out of her stupor, hiding her face behind her own drink as she took a sip. She was no better than the other women in town, was she? There was no denying that Sam had a certain appeal, but she'd always prided herself on being immune to such things. She'd always been a "keep your eye on the prize" kind of girl—that philosophy had held her in good stead through many, many difficult years.

And so it would now, too. Besides, Sam wasn't interested in her. He'd made enough disparaging comments during their first few meetings for her to know that she was not his type.

"Thanks, that hits the spot," he said, leaning against the porch post.

"I finished my sewing and thought you might be thirsty," she replied. She'd just go inside now before she embarrassed herself. She consoled her pride with the fact that she was human, after all, and her eyes were in perfect working order. It was nothing more than that. She turned on her heel but his voice stopped her.

"Stay. The boards are sound now and I dusted the cobwebs off the chairs."

The invitation was tempting. Sitting in the warm purple twilight with Sam Diamond and sipping tart lemonade sounded like a good way to end the day. Too good. "That's okay. I still have things to finish up inside."

She dared look up at him, and she was surprised to see concern softening his hard features.

"You've been burning the candle at both ends." He moved his hand, gesturing at the chair. "Let it wait until tomorrow."

She raised an eyebrow. Did he want to spend time with her? Had he cleaned off the chairs for this specific reason? Her heart sped up thinking about it. Besides, Sam was a bit of pot calling kettle. "Would you leave it 'til tomorrow if you had things left to do?"

Delicious crinkles formed at the corners of his

eyes as he gave a small smile of acquiescence. "Touché."

But he was right, she admitted to herself. She had been working hard and she knew part of her sewing trouble had come from being tired and inattentive. "Well, maybe just for a minute."

She took her glass and sat in one of the Adirondack chairs, letting out a sigh as she sank into the curved wooden back. They needed scraping and repainting like everything else, but for right now it was perfect. Sam likewise sat, took off his hat, and stretched out his impossibly long legs. He took a sip of what was left of his lemonade and turned his head to look at her.

"Can I ask you a question?"

A mourning dove set up a lonely call and Angela rested her head against the chair. "It depends."

"Is this project personal for you?"

She turned her head and studied his face. When his gaze met hers, she knew. He'd guessed. The invitation to sit had been deliberate, she knew that now. And she was scrambling to come up with an appropriate answer that would appease him and yet tell him nothing. Her hesitation spun out, weaving a web around them consisting of what she didn't say rather than what she did.

Finally she sighed. "Of course it is. I've put a lot of energy into it. I couldn't have done that if I weren't committed to its success."

Sam put his glass on the arm of the chair. "That's not what I meant."

"I know," she admitted, meeting his gaze.

"The other day, when I grabbed your arm..."

She saw his Adam's apple bob as he swallowed. A sinking feeling weighed down her chest. Was that why he was here tonight? Guilt?

"Don't worry about it," she murmured, lowering her eyes.

"I can't stop thinking about it." His voice was husky now in the semi-darkness and it sneaked past her defenses, making her vulnerable. She didn't want him to care. Didn't need him to. And yet it felt nice to have someone see beyond the image she showed the world every day.

"All the color drained from your face, and your eyes..." He cleared his throat. "You recovered quickly, but not before I saw. And it suddenly made sense. I'm sorry, Angela. I never meant to frighten you."

He met her gaze fully now, and she was surprised at the honesty in his eyes. He looked different without his hat—more approachable, more casual. Probably too casual to be sitting here alone with her. And now they were sharing something. It created an intimacy that felt a little too good. It would be so much easier if she could simply treat Sam like a client! She never lost her objectivity with clients.

"Is that why you came back? Because you feel guilty? Because it was nothing, Sam, really."

He hesitated. "It made me think about what you said about the foundation, that's all. Put it… Well, put it into context, I suppose."

It was a good answer and Angela leaned her head back against the chair. It felt odd to be talking and not butting heads, but good. It was progress. His voice was quiet and hopeful and it touched Angela's heart. She'd accused him of not wanting to face the ugliness of life, but here he was anyway. On some level he cared.

But could he handle her personal "context"? She doubted it. Nor did she care to tell it, so she tailored her response to satisfy his curiosity while only truly skimming the surface. She didn't want to go all the way back. Not ever.

"Before I became a social worker, I found myself in a bad situation, yes. But I left. So you see I'm not so bad off after all. You just took me by surprise the other day.

"Did he…you know. Hit you?" He struggled over the words.

How to answer? Her story was not simple or easy. She could see where his assumptions were leading him and it was probably the easiest, cleanest way out. "Once," she admitted, hearing the crack in her voice. She cleared her throat. "It had been bad for a while, but after he hit me I left."

It barely scratched the surface of her tangled history but it did the trick. "So when I grabbed your wrist…it was thoughtless, Angela. I'm sorry."

"It was the reaction of a moment. And already forgotten. Don't worry about it." She tried a smile that didn't quite feel genuine.

"I'm glad," he replied. "The last thing I'd want to do is…"

He let the thought trail off, but it didn't matter. She understood. This was a different Sam and Angela wasn't sure what to do with the change. Being aware of his physical attributes was one thing. But starting to *like* him? Bad news. All the same, she needed him as an ally. She wanted to trust him—especially this Sam, who was currently without the self-important edge she'd sensed from him at the beginning. A man who was thoughtful and caring.

But she didn't want to be the foundation's poster child. Rather she wanted him to make the connection to the women who would call this place home. She felt a moment of sadness, wishing her mother could be one of those women. She knew it would never happen, but she couldn't extinguish the tiny spark of hope that still flared from time to time.

"The women coming here have gone through the hardest part—leaving their particular situation. Now they're ready to rebuild their lives and need a nudge and helping hand to get started. Our first resident is already lined up. Once she's settled our first task will be to help her find a job. When our residents are on their way to a new life, then they'll go out on their own."

"Like a butterfly out of a cocoon."

"Yes, exactly like that." She smiled, glad he'd connected the dots. "We hope they'll leave with a little cash in their pockets, as well as some confidence and hope for the future."

Silence fell for a few minutes as the shadows deepened. Angela sipped her drink while they watched a pair of squirrels race through the yard and up a poplar tree. She was ever aware of Sam sitting next to her, the length of his long, strong legs, the way his T-shirt sleeves revealed tanned, strong forearms. He'd reached out tonight. Nothing could have surprised—or pleased—her more. Even if it had cost her a corner of her privacy.

"It's a good program," he admitted.

Sam was saying all the right things, but there was a little voice in the back of her head saying that she shouldn't be too quick to believe. All her training, all her life experience had taught her that she had to be clear-headed and objective. To feel compassion and a need to help, but not to insert her personal feelings into a situation.

"This situation," Sam said carefully, "was he your husband?"

"No," she replied, making the word deliberately definite so as to close the subject. She kept her private life private. She'd learned to be skeptical years ago, somewhere between the fear and the anger. Home life had been frightening and fraught with anxiety. Sam's question made her feel that he could somehow see right past her barriers and it made her uneasy. No one needed to know how personal this cause truly was to her heart. How close she'd come to history repeating itself before she got out.

She couldn't meet his eyes now. She'd always made a point of judging what she saw, but she hadn't with Sam. She'd formed an opinion because of things she'd heard and then read that into her impression of him rather than giving him the benefit of the doubt. She didn't very much like what that said about her.

Sam watched Angela lower her eyes. He knew very well he hadn't made a good impression the first few times they'd met, but he was trying to make up for it. His reasons for being abrasive in the beginning had been his own stress talking. But his sincere questions tonight had taken the snap and sparkle out of her eyes. He found he missed it.

"You're doing a good thing here, Angela."

"I'm pleased you think so." She looked up briefly.

"I'm not a liar, and I wasn't trying to be mean

before. I do have my hands full—we're trying to finalize details on a biogas facility at the ranch. Let's just say it hasn't gone as smoothly as I'd like. I haven't had many moments to spare. I probably could have been more tactful." He offered a smile, hoping to change the subject. He didn't like seeing her look so sad.

"Biogas?"

Gratified she'd taken the bait, he continued. "We can turn our organic waste into energy. Specifically, enough energy to run our entire operation and then some without touching the power grid. But it's newer technology and it doesn't come cheap." Even talking about it made him excited. The initial capital was what his father kept harping on, but Sam knew their coffers could take it. The reason for his dad's worry he suspected was not as black and white and had to be handled more delicately. And Sam wasn't used to dealing that way. There'd been a lot of adjustments since his father's sudden illness.

"You? A 'green' farmer? I never would have guessed it."

"I get the feeling that you formed a lot of opinions about me that may turn out to be wrong."

She blushed a little and he watched the way the breeze ruffled her hair in the increasing darkness. The last of the June bugs were starting to hit the porch door as the light from within glowed through the rectangular window.

"Our ranch has been in the family for generations. Each new generation bears a responsibility—to the family, to the land. I'm nothing but a steward, until…"

"Until the next generation? But aren't you an only child?"

He rested his elbows on his knees. "Yep."

It was the one way he knew he'd disappointed the family, but he refused to enter into a marriage that wasn't real, that wasn't based on love and respect. He was probably foolish and an idealist, but that was where he drew the line. He imagined admitting such a thing to Angela. He suspected she'd laugh in his face. It was rather sentimental, he supposed. He wanted the kind of marriage his parents had.

The only reason he hadn't pushed harder about the development was that Virgil's stroke had made Sam suddenly aware of the fact that his dad—who'd always seemed invincible—wouldn't always be there with him. Coming to terms with that was a hard pill to swallow.

"You've gone quiet all of a sudden."

He smacked his hands on his knees and pushed himself to standing. "Just tired. I should get a move on." *Before I say too much*, he thought. He was finding her far too easy to talk to.

"I appreciate the help tonight, Sam. I know you're busy."

He chuckled. "That must have been hard for you to say."

"Maybe a little." Her lips twitched. "I probably haven't been entirely fair. If we hadn't sent out press releases and set up media…"

"It's okay. I handed off a few things to my foreman. It's a few days, nothing more. I'll manage."

Angela drained what was left of the lemonade from her glass and stood up. "Well, thanks for coming. At least I won't have to worry about anyone falling through the porch on Saturday."

"No problem." He picked up his glass and followed her into the house. He put it in the sink as Angela draped the blue curtains over her arm. "You don't have more to do?" he said, hooking his thumbs in his pockets.

"Just hang these curtains. I have to put them up tonight because I don't want to fold them and crease the fabric, and I can't leave them out or Morris will be sure to have fun playing in the material hanging over the ironing board."

Ah, the devilish Morris. Sam figured he should consider it an achievement that he'd gone from being bitten to simply being ignored. The cat was nowhere to be seen. "I'll give you a hand."

"No, really…"

"Which room?"

She met his gaze and he knew she was exhausted when she gave in without too much of a fight. "Upstairs, first door on the left."

CHAPTER FIVE

ANGELA followed Sam up the stairs, staying a few steps behind and trying to avoid looking at the worn patches on his jeans. She failed utterly. They'd learned more about each other tonight and it had created some common ground—ground that Angela wasn't sure she was comfortable treading. He was far harder to dismiss when he was like this.

"Do you have the rods installed?" Sam's deep voice shimmered in the darkness of the stairway. How he could sound so good saying something so banal was impressive. She pushed the reaction to the side and told herself to remain focused on practicalities.

"They're not up yet. They're ready though, and my tool box is in the closet." They reached the landing and Angela let out a sigh of relief as they emerged from the confined space of the stairway. "Here we are. Hang on and I'll flip on a light. The last bracket I installed I made a mess of and had to fix the drywall."

They stepped inside the room and she hit the switch. Light from the overhead fixture lit up the room and she looked at Sam, standing there with soft blue fabric draped over his arms. It looked out of place against his tanned masculinity, and the effect of the contrast was appealing. She paused to enjoy the picture. She might be immune to his charms but she could still appreciate his finer points. And they were *very* fine.

"Let me take those from you," she murmured. "This will only take a minute or two."

She moved to take the panels from his arms and as he slipped them into her hands their fingers touched. His were warm and rough and it tripped her personal distance alarm big-time. The tips of his fingers grazed the inside of her wrist and butterflies winged their way through her stomach as she snatched her fingers away.

Okay. The last thing she expected to feel around Sam Diamond was this flicker of physical awareness. She slid the fabric the rest of the way out of his hands and stepped back. She wasn't sure if he had touched her deliberately or not. But she was positive of one thing. He couldn't ever know that he affected her in any way. She simply didn't *do* touching. It hit too many triggers.

Instead she inhaled, and counted to ten as she exhaled.

Sam didn't seem to notice her reaction; instead

he looked around the room. Angela felt an expanding sense of pride. "It's pretty, isn't it?" she asked, seeking level emotional ground again.

"The color—it looks like something my mother would pick out. Like the old chinaware she's got."

Angela smiled. "She did pick out the color, and the material, too. I think it's kind of classic, don't you?"

"She's classic," he replied, smiling, and Angela tried to ignore the way his eyes warmed when he spoke about Molly. Sam was clearly devoted to his mama, and he always spoke of her with love and respect. But Angela had to wonder if there was a reason why someone as handsome and well-established as Sam hadn't been snapped up off the market? He was a good-looking, successful guy. Amy had said that he'd given her a line about not wanting to lead her on and give her false expectations and made it sound as if it was merely an excuse to be rid of her. Angela now wondered if he'd been sincere while ending the relationship, and if the wonderful example Molly set had created a standard that other women simply couldn't live up to.

Not that she was inclined to try to reach the mark herself. She'd never really bought into that idea of married bliss, two halves of one whole and the whole nine yards. So far she'd done just fine on her own.

"Well, the curtains are the finishing touch. Shall

we?" She nodded toward the two large windows on the north wall, suddenly impatient to see the final effect. Looking around the room, she was struck once more with a sense of satisfaction. She'd done a good job here if she did say so herself. The hardwood only needed a good cleaning and polishing and then Angela was leaving the room be. The women would want to put their things there, make the space their own. She knew very well how important it felt to have a say. For years she'd been forced to keep her room just so. She'd longed to change the paper, the color, put things on the walls. None of it was allowed. She'd never been able to have anything that smacked of individuality. But the residents here deserved a room of their own for the duration of their stay, and she was determined that they would get it.

"The rods are in the closet. Just a sec." She laid the curtains over the bed and went to get the café rods and her toolbox. In a few short minutes Sam had measured, marked and screwed the brackets to the wall. Angela slid the tabs over the rod and stood on tiptoe, arms above her head, holding it steady while Sam threaded the rod through the hole and screwed the decorative finial on the end. As he reached to do the other side, his hands slid over hers. The electricity from the touch rocketed through Angela's body and she lowered her hands quickly, stepping away from the window. That wasn't supposed to happen again!

This reaction—this attraction—was just wrong on so many levels. She didn't even want to like him, let alone feel…what was it she was feeling, anyway? Desire? It couldn't be. Desire meant wanting, and she didn't want this. She didn't know what to do with it.

It was just some weird chemistry thing. It must be, because nothing like this had ever happened to her before. Touches, even simple ones, always made her want to shy away. But Sam's left her wanting more and that scared her to death.

And there was still another curtain to contend with.

There was no sound in the room now and it put Angela more on edge. Did he know what he was doing to her? Was he playing a game? The moments ticked by and she wished he'd say something. If he provoked her she could at least respond. As it was she was beginning to think that he'd felt it too. Heavens, one of them being jumpy was enough. It was easier to deal with him when he was teasing or baiting her. In the silence her body still hummed from the innocent contact.

It was akin to torture to lift her arms again, holding the rod while he threaded it through the first side. She inhaled a shaky breath, Sam looked down at her, and the finial dropped to the floor and rolled a few feet away.

"Hang on," he said, his voice soft and husky. She stood, frozen to the spot while he retrieved the curled knob, and when he came back to put the second end through the bracket he stood behind her, his hands raised above hers as he reached for the rod.

His chest pressed gently against her back and she shivered, aware that with her arms up her breasts were very accessible. All he'd have to do was slide his hands down over her shoulders and he could be touching her. There was a pause—just a breath— but she was as aware of a man's body as she'd ever been. She was trapped in the circle of his arms, blocked by his body, telling herself she had no reason to be afraid and yet trembling just the same. There was an intimacy here that she wasn't prepared for. And yet neither of them had spoken a word or made an overt move.

She couldn't breathe. She had to get out of here, get away from the hard warmth of his body and his scent...oh, for goodness' sake, when did the smell of fresh-cut lumber and lemon become so appealing? "Have you got it?" she asked, hoping her voice didn't sound as shaky as she felt.

"I've got it," he replied.

She let go of the curtain rod as though it was burning her hands and slid out from beneath his arm. The air around her cooled and she exhaled with relief. What surprised her most was the empty sense of disappointment that rushed in where moments ago desire and fear had battled.

He cleared his throat and resumed screwing the finials on the rod as if nothing had happened. When he was done, he smoothed out the panel so that it lay flat. "There you go," he said, turning around.

When she looked at him something seemed to snap in the air between them. All it would take was one step and she could feel the heat of his body again. One step and she could explore the sensations that rocketed through her body when he was near. She saw his eyes widen as the moment spun out and the air seemed to ripple between them. He was so powerful, so forceful without any effort, and Angela knew he could swallow up a little wallflower like her in the blink of an eye.

"That's unexpected," he acknowledged quietly, and Angela wished he'd never spoken at all.

"I don't know what you mean," she countered, picking up the screwdriver and dropping it in the toolbox, hoping it would put him off. Being close to him set off tons of personal boundary alarms, but the truly terrifying thing for Angela was her own betraying reaction to him. She was back to not trusting herself or her judgment, and it made her stomach twist sickeningly. She'd made too many mistakes to risk making another.

"I mean whatever it was that just happened." He pursued the subject, and she wished he'd just shut up and let the matter drop. "And it obviously scares you to death. I suppose, considering your past..."

She forced herself to face him, schooling her features into what she hoped was an unreadable mask. This was why she didn't talk about her own history. Suddenly it defined her and everything she did. "All that happened here is that you helped me install some curtain rods. And that's all that can happen, Mr. Diamond," she added significantly.

The corner of his mouth turned up. "So we're back to Mr. Diamond again. You're plenty rattled."

"Are there no bounds to your ego?" She snapped out the question, but it stung because he was one-hundred-percent right. Had he provoked her deliberately in those long moments when he'd let his chest ride so close to her back? She didn't want to think so. Whether it had been intentional or not, she'd fallen for it. She straightened her spine. Now she felt vulnerable *and* ridiculous, not to mention transparent. "I appreciate all of your help with the project, but if you're looking for more than that..."

"Ms. Beck." He took a step closer and her heart started beating strangely again. "I have just about all I can handle with Diamondback and my other commitments. I'm not 'looking for' anything."

"Then..."

The rest of the question was silently asked. What was going on between them? The pause deepened and so did his dimple. "What do *you* propose we do about it?"

"Do about it?" There was a definite squeak in her voice now and she wasn't sure if it was fear or anticipation. She cleared her throat. "We don't do anything. You're the one playing games, Sam."

"I don't play games," he replied, standing taller. "You don't strike me as someone into casual relationships, Angela." His smile faded. "And I'm not looking for anything serious. So that pretty much takes care of that, right? We'll just forget it ever happened."

"Right," she parroted, so completely off balance now she wasn't entirely sure what he was saying and what he wasn't. She didn't do casual relationships because she didn't do *any* relationships. She could never let anyone close enough. Not that he needed to know that.

"Now if you'll excuse me, it's getting late and I'm sure we both need our rest."

"Of course."

He brushed by her. Moments later she heard his truck door slam and the engine start. She sagged, resting her flaming cheek against the cool blue wall, watching through the window as he drove away.

He'd been utterly sincere in his last words. So

why didn't Angela quite believe him? He'd certainly been in an all-fired hurry to leave.

He was right about one thing—she was dog-tired. But she suspected sleep would be a long time coming tonight. Sam Diamond had a way of challenging everything. And what freaked her out the most was realizing that even knowing her past, he hadn't run. She had.

Sam pushed his mount harder over the trail, enjoying the feel of the wide-open gallop and the wind on his face. Nothing had prepared him for the jolt he'd suffered the moment his body had touched Angela's. And then she'd had the nerve to accuse him of playing games.

It had bothered him ever since he'd left her standing in the bedroom, her face pale and her greeny-blue eyes huge as they stared at him. He couldn't get her off his mind. He could still see the spark in her eyes. He'd seen something else, too—fear. She was afraid of him and he'd had the strangest desire to pull her into his arms and tell her it was all right.

Knowing her past, though, made him question every action, wondering how it would appear to her. So instead of following his instincts, he'd got himself out of there. Angela wasn't a woman he could trifle with. And anything more than trifling scared him witless.

To top it off, his father had truly dug in his heels about the biogas facility, flat-out refusing to sign any papers so they could release the money and begin construction. Sam had been so angry he'd nearly yelled at Virgil—a man still recovering from a stroke. He'd managed to hold on to his temper, but it had only taken one small mention of Power of Attorney and Virgil's eyes had blazed at him. Despite his verbal difficulties he had very clearly made his point as he shouted, "Not crazy!"

Sam had slammed out the door instead, deciding that a good, old-fashioned hell-bent-for-leather ride was in order to work off the tension. Nothing was going right. Everything felt unsettled and off balance. Every attempt he made at holding the family together was a flop. He'd come terribly close to telling his father to start walking and get back where he belonged, but he'd reined in his emotions. It wasn't Virgil's fault. It wasn't anyone's fault. They were all just trying to cope the best they knew how.

His horse started to lather and Sam knew he couldn't push him any harder.

As he started over the crest of the hill, Sam stared at the flat parcel of land marked with surveyor's stakes. Seeing it waiting, so empty and perfect, made his shoulders tense. He was a grown man, for God's sake. A man who could make his own decisions, not a boy beneath his father's thumb.

The whole issue made him feel impotent and ineffectual. Was this how Ty had felt before he'd taken off for parts unknown? Once more Sam wished his cousin were here to talk things over with. It wasn't the same with him gone.

The more nagging problem was that he was still thinking about Angela. That wasn't a good sign.

He slowed and let the gelding walk, the restlessness unabated in himself. He remembered the guarded look on her face as she'd admitted she'd gotten out of a bad relationship. Something had happened in that moment. More than knowledge—he'd guessed as much when she'd blanched after he'd grabbed her wrist. It was something else.

It was trust. And the moment in the bedroom had taken that delicate trust and shattered it. Maybe she was right. Maybe he had played games because he'd indulged in the attraction even knowing their connection was fragile at best.

He dug his heels into the gelding's side. He needed to get away from here for a while, clear his head. The least he could do was make it up to her, right?

Angela counted down the hours. Less than twenty-four now and everyone would be here. A reporter and photographer from the local paper, someone from the town council, even the Member of the Legislature was slated to attend. The very idea of being front and center made her lightheaded with dread, but she reminded herself that it was part of her job. And with Sam here, she could stay under the radar.

The more important problem was that she didn't even have a chair for them to sit on beyond the somewhat scarred table and chairs in the kitchen. Somehow she had to get the sofa and chairs from the garage into the living room without scuffing the new floor.

She was struggling with the first armchair when she heard the steady growl of a truck engine. She peered over the top of the chair and saw Sam's face behind the wheel, cowboy hat and sunglasses shading his face. Her heart began pounding and she nearly dropped the chair. What was he doing here? After the curtain incident she'd been sure he wouldn't be back. And she'd considered that just as well.

He got out of the truck, shut the door, and took off the glasses, letting them dangle from one hand for a moment before folding them up and tucking them into the neck of his shirt. Oh, boy. He was Trouble with a capital *T.* Maybe he'd shown a softer side the other night, but it hadn't exactly ended well. So what was he doing back here?

He knocked on the screen door as Angela's arms started to scream in protest. She waddled the half-dozen steps it took to get into the living room and put the chair down as Sam called, "Angela?"

She brushed her hands off and walked to the door, trying to steady her pace and her pulse. "Sam. What on earth?"

"It occurred to me you might be a bit short-handed trying to get ready for tomorrow."

Shorthanded. So he was only here to help? She paused, torn between needing his help and needing to be honest. "You left in an awful hurry the other night. I didn't expect to see you until tomorrow."

He looked at her through the screen door, watching her steadily and making her feel about two inches tall. How could she turn away a pair of willing, strong hands?

He held out the appendages in question. "And yet here I am."

"Aren't you too busy at Diamondback?"

"I needed to get away for a bit. Got in the truck and ended up here, thinking you might be able to put me to work."

"I…uh…see."

Oh, brilliant response, Angela, she thought, shifting her weight on her feet nervously. Having him show up while she was thinking about him didn't help matters at all.

One eyebrow raised. "Are you going to talk to me through this screen door all day?"

She sighed. Of course not. She was ashamed to admit that she was far more concerned with her own behavior than his. As the social worker, she was supposed to be the well-adjusted one, so Sam could never know about all the unresolved feelings he stirred up. "No funny business," she said, opening the door and inviting him in.

He burst out laughing. "Funny business?"

Her face heated. Despite her intentions to the contrary, she was making a fool of herself. "Oh, never mind. I do need help so don't say you weren't warned." He couldn't be that much trouble with six feet and a hundred pounds of sofa between them, could he? That little atmospheric moment was a one-off. "I was wondering how I was going to get the furniture moved in from the garage." A perfectly good, safe activity.

"The boys could have done it tomorrow."

"That's what I originally decided. But then I thought, what if it rains? And people are coming. I need somewhere for them to sit if we can't be outdoors, right?"

He looked into the empty living room and back to her again, his eyes disapproving. She knew it was silly to think of doing it all herself. And she hated that she somehow felt she needed his approval when she didn't.

"You should have called."

"So you could have said you were too busy? No thanks."

His eyes widened with surprise at her quick response, and then seemed to warm with a new respect. "You know, sometimes it beats me why I keep coming back here."

"Maybe you're a sucker for punishment." She tilted her chin. Enough was enough. She kept letting him get the upper hand and it was time that changed. At the same time, there was a new edge to the words now. Not the angry, spiteful edge that had been prevalent in their first meetings. But something else. It almost felt like teasing. Banter. Right now he was looking at her like he was up to something. The boyish expression made him look younger than she expected he was and very, very sexy.

"Maybe I am," he replied slowly, and punctuated it with a wink.

Angela burst out laughing. "Okay, you had me until the wink. Seriously?"

Sam shoved his hands in his pockets. "Over the top?"

"Yeah. A bit."

"Then I'd better stop making a fool of myself and get to work, huh?"

She led him to the garage while a new, unfamiliar warmth expanded inside her. It was a surprise to find that she was slowly growing to trust Sam. How could her first impression have been so wrong? She'd thought him all swagger and arrogance, but there was more to Sam Diamond than what she'd first thought was a huge sense of self-entitlement. He had a generous spirit and a sense of humor, the humble kind that meant he didn't mind poking fun at himself a little. She'd been wrong to accuse him of ego. What had happened was as much her fault as his.

As he lifted the other wing chair effortlessly, Angela swallowed, staring at the way the fabric of his shirt stretched across the muscles of his chest and arms. It was just as well that the project was getting closer to launch. Once things were underway their paths would rarely need to cross. Perhaps a chance encounter in town, or at a board meeting of the foundation.

Besides, after Butterfly House was well-established, she had plans. If she had her way, there'd be several houses like this one scattered around the country. It was going to take all her energy to make that a reality. There wasn't room for sexy distractions in those plans.

While Sam took the chair inside, she grabbed an end table and followed him. Together they positioned the chairs and put the table between, and Angela brought out a lamp to place upon it. It made the corner of the room cozy. Next they manhandled the sofa.

"We're not going to trip over your cat, are we?" he asked, puffing a little as they hefted it up.

"He's been hiding in the basement most of the day. I think you're safe."

"Okay, now tilt it a little," Sam suggested, "to fit the arms through the doorway."

It was heavy and Angela braced the weight against her knee as she fought for a better grip and turned it slightly for a better angle. "Easy for you to say."

"Shout if you have to put it down."

As if. Her competitive spirit rose up and made her determined to carry her weight. She gave the sofa a boost and said, "I'm fine. Go."

It wasn't done gracefully, but they managed to get the sofa into the living room and put into place without scratching the new finish on the floor. "It's starting to look like a room," she said, brushing off her hands.

"What's left?"

There were two footstools and a coffee table still in the garage, and within moments they had the room organized. A quick polish and vacuum and it would be fine.

Angela looked at Sam. He'd left his customary hat on the coatrack by the door and his hair was slightly mussed and damp from lifting in the July heat. She looked down at herself—a smear of dust streaked across her left breast, light beige against the navy T-shirt. She dusted it off and rubbed her hands on her jeans. The room was done but she didn't want him to leave yet. She'd have too much time on her hands to fuss and flutter and worry about all the things that could go wrong tomorrow. Sam made her focus on other things.

"There's a mattress and box spring that just arrived yesterday," she piped up. "I don't suppose you'd care to help me get them up the stairs?"

"Sure. Might as well use me while I'm here."

"Use him" indeed. Angela ignored the rush of heat at his innocently spoken words. They took the mattress up first and leaned it against the wall of the sunny yellow room. The box spring was harder to manage. The rigid frame made it unwieldy to get around the corner of the stairs, and it took three tries to get the angle lined up correctly to get it through the door of the bedroom. Angela's face was flushed and her breath was labored as they finally got inside and shifted the box spring so that they could lay it on the bed frame she'd put together. She nearly had it when the corner slipped and it started to slide. A splinter from the wood dug into her finger and she let go as a reflex.

"Ow!"

Sam's face flattened in alarm as he tried to take as much weight of the box spring as possible, but it was too unbalanced. It tipped and dropped, landing squarely on her toes.

"Oh!" There was a sharp pain in her big toe that began radiating out in waves. Despite the splinter, she bent to lift the box spring off her foot as her eyes watered. She took a step toward the bed and gasped out a curse.

"Put it down," Sam instructed. "Just lay it down, Angela. I'll put it on the frame later."

They laid it across the frame and she exhaled fully as Sam rushed around the corner of the bed. "Did you break it? I thought you had it…"

"I did have it, until this." She held up her hand with the splinter still sticking out.

"Let me have a look."

She wasn't about to argue, and held up her hand for his examination.

"You should sit down," he suggested, looking into her face. She tried not to wince but wasn't entirely sure she was succeeding.

The pain in her toe was horrible and she wanted nothing more than to get off her feet. But there was nowhere to sit in the bedroom. "We'll have to go downstairs."

"Come on, then. Put your arm around my neck."

She looked at him, so shocked at his suggestion that she temporarily forgot about her toe and splinter. What would it be like to be picked up off her feet and held against his wide chest with his strong arms? It made something inside her lift up and go all fizzy. She couldn't quite make the leap between the idea and actual physical contact, though. Oh, how she wished she were one of those confident women who could slide their arms around a handsome man and be comfortable doing so. Instead Angela felt a cloying sense of claustrophobia, as if she were pinned—a butterfly under glass, vulnerable and unable to escape.

She shook her head. "That's okay. I can walk."

She hobbled to the stairs and used the banister for support as she made her way down the steps one by one. She refused to look at Sam, who stayed beside her on each step. She appreciated the solicitude but he was too close and she was too aware of his body blocking her against the stairway. At the bottom she grimaced but refused his arm when he offered it.

"Stubborn as a mule," he muttered, following her into the living room.

She sank into the chair. "You got that right. Did you forget?"

"I guess I must have." He was looking at her with concern and it made the parts of her that weren't throbbing with pain go all squishy. It was inconceivable that he might actually care about her, wasn't it? It was only a few weeks ago that he'd pointed a finger at her in the boardroom in Edmonton and told her not to expect a thing from him.

And now here he was. Doing a very good impression of being there for her and she was afraid she might be getting used to it.

The pain wasn't so bad now that she was off her feet and she sighed. This was just what she needed. How was she going to supervise a dozen energetic teens tomorrow if she could hardly hobble from one room to the next? Tears of frustration stung her eyes as she contemplated the to-do list. She hadn't even begun on the refreshments yet…

"Do you think it's broken?"

"I don't know. I hope not."

Sam's troubled gaze met hers, and then he reached in his pocket. He took out a Swiss army knife and plucked out a set of tweezers. "Let's see your hand first," he said, pulling over a foot stool and sitting on it. She held out her hand and winced as he gently squeezed the skin around the splinter. With a few quick plucks she felt the wood slide out of her skin. "It's a good one, but it's out."

"Thanks," she replied. And was going to say more but realized that Sam's hands were on her ankle, lifting her leg to rest across his knee.

"Let's have a look at that toe," he said quietly.

She held her breath as his warm hands circled her ankle and carefully removed her shoe and rolled her sock down over her heel. Every nerve ending in her body was aware of his gentle touch and she bit down on her lip. She could do this. She could handle being touched, even if it did feel far too intimate. The sock slid off into his fingers and he dropped it on the floor. His careful examination was intensely uncomfortable—a mix of shooting pain, uneasiness at the personal nature of his probing and delicious pleasure as he touched gently with his fingers. His thumb was along her instep and rubbed the arch as he turned her foot. It felt wonderful and she relaxed against the back of the chair.

"You've bruised it good," he said quietly. "I don't think it's broken. Even if it is, there's not much you can do for it but stay off it. We should try to get the swelling down, though. Got any ice?"

"There's an ice pack in the kitchen freezer," she said, and watched with her senses clamoring as he put her foot carefully on the footstool and disappeared, only to return a moment later with the pack wrapped in a dish towel.

"You need to keep it elevated and the ice on it. Take some ibuprofen. It's an anti-inflammatory."

"I don't have any. I have a policy about not keeping any drugs in the house, even over-the-counter ones." She had a first aid kit but no medication.

"Then I'll go get you some."

She leaned back against the chair, finally admitting defeat. Up until now she'd been sure she could have everything put together. She couldn't now.

She was going to look like an amateur.

Her bottom lip wobbled. Just a little, and she

sucked it up, but not in time. Sam's brows pulled together.

"What is it?"

"There's no way I'll be ready now. I have reporters and politicians coming—" that very thought caused her heart to stutter "—and a dusty living room and no food. I have a dozen teens coming from the youth center to do yard work, and how am I going to supervise if I can't even walk around the property?"

She felt so very vulnerable, and it was truly a bad state of affairs if she was confiding in Sam Diamond. The last time she'd given him a personal glimpse it hadn't turned him away as she'd expected.

"It'll be ready, I promise."

"Please don't make promises you can't keep, Sam. I can't bear it."

She'd heard too many promises, had too many broken over the years, especially by people she was supposed to trust. She'd heard a lot of apologies, all of them sincerely meant. And then she'd felt the blistering rage when something didn't go her father's way. She'd heard it all from Steve, too, until one day he'd backhanded her across the face.

He'd done her a favor because that was the day she broke free of the pattern forever.

But she didn't believe in promises and assurances. Not even from someone like Sam.

"I do not make idle promises. I'll be honest and walk away before breaking my word."

Her heart surged at the sincerity in his voice. She *wanted* to believe him. So badly.

"Sam, I..." Her throat thickened. She didn't want to depend on him to make this right. She didn't want to depend on anyone.

"Hush," he said, bending over and putting his hands on the arm of the chair. "You'll have everything you need. It'll go off without a hitch. Can you trust me?"

His eyes searched hers and she noticed tiny gold flecks in the irises. He was asking her to trust him with Butterfly House, the one thing she cared about most. Could she? She wanted to. She wanted to so badly it hurt inside. But she was afraid—of everything he was making her feel. Her hesitation was slowly melting away—the armor that she'd used to protect herself for years. In its absence came a whole host of other problems. She had no idea how to handle a situation like this.

But in the end she had no choice. She lifted her eyes to his and took a breath. "Yes," she breathed. "I trust you."

There was a long moment where their eyes met, accepted. And then Sam leaned in and did the one thing she feared and longed for most: he kissed her.

CHAPTER SIX

ANGELA'S heart skidded as his lips touched hers.
She wasn't prepared for how they'd feel—gentle,
warm and seductive. She remembered reading a
book once where a character described kissing the
hero as feeling like sliding down a rainbow. Angela
had thought it a silly comparison at the time. Now
she understood what it meant. It was *heavenly*.

She sighed a little as his mouth nibbled at hers,
teasing and making her forget all about her throbbing toe. Hesitantly she responded, not quite comfortable with the intimacy of it all but wooed just
the same. There were no demands made. There
was only the whisper of his lips on hers. How long
had it been since she'd been kissed this way? Had
she ever been? It was as if he somehow knew she
needed patience and tenderness.

But when his hand slipped from the arm of the
chair to her shoulder, she pulled away, breaking the
contact. This couldn't happen. She couldn't let him
this close. For a tense second their mouths seemed

to hover, only scant inches apart. Then, to her surprise, he leaned his forehead against hers. There was an openness in the gesture that surprised and touched her. Where was the irascible rancher she'd butted heads with at the beginning? The man who'd claimed he didn't have time for her or her cause? She knew he was still in there somewhere.

The most worrying thing was that she liked this new side of Sam. When was the last time she'd felt pretty, desirable, cared for? He made her feel all those things and more, without the crippling anxiety that usually accompanied any sort of romantic overture.

"I'm sorry, Angela. I wasn't going to do that today."

Today. Nerves bubbled up as she realized his words confirmed that he'd thought about it before. When? When they were hanging the curtains? Drinking lemonade on the porch? Arguing at Diamondback? She swallowed. It might have been easier to pass off if it had just been a spur-of-the-moment impulse. But knowing he'd considered doing it—that he'd ostensibly told himself he wasn't going to kiss her and now had—that changed things.

Something was going on between them, something bigger than she was comfortable with. Was he interested in a relationship? That was impossible. He'd made it very plain he didn't have time for romance.

"Then why did you?"

He squatted down beside the chair, leaving his hands on the arms. "Maybe because today you were human. Today you admitted defeat. I know how hard that was for you to do. I know what it cost you." He sighed. "Boy, do I know."

She swiped her tongue over her lips; now they held the tang of bitterness. Why did she have to fail in order to be attractive to him? She never wanted anyone to pity her ever again. She'd come too far for that. "You felt sorry for me."

"No!" He shook his head. "For the first time, the cold veneer you wear all the time slipped."

Was that how he saw her? Cold? She curled her arms around her middle. Is that how *everyone* saw her? She knew she was focused and she was guarded. She had been wary of letting anyone in, giving them any power over her at all. She refused to be beneath anyone's thumb the way she'd been under her father's. Every insult and slap had eroded her childish confidence bit by bit until she'd nearly believed she was nothing. She'd had to fight her way back. But this was the first time she'd really sat back and thought about how she must appear to others. Each time she saw a neglected child or a woman who'd lost her hope for the future, her heart broke a little more. If she appeared that way it was because she refused to let her compassion be a weakness for someone to exploit.

"I don't trust easily, that's all," she said quietly, wanting to explain in some small way. "When you trust someone and they betray that trust… I don't mean to be cold. Just careful."

She couldn't explain it any better than that. She didn't trust anyone with her secrets. She supposed being considered aloof was a small price to pay for her privacy.

"And you don't trust me, either, do you?" He frowned.

"I don't want to, no."

He got up and lifted her foot so he could sit on the footstool again, putting her feet on his thighs. "That implies that you do, on some level."

Angela closed her eyes briefly. She didn't want to have this conversation. She wished Molly had never stepped away from the board. As exciting as Sam could be, he complicated things. He managed to see her the way no one had seen her before and that was terrifying. The truth was ugly.

"You don't even want to be here. You said so," she defended. "And you keep coming back. You said you don't want anything romantic." She forced herself to say the word; they'd just kissed so it wasn't as if it was taboo now. "And now you're here and you're kissing me. What do you want, Sam? Because I can't keep up with your mixed signals."

"I want to help." His hand rested warmly on her ankle and she fought not to pull away from what he probably considered a casual touch but what meant so much more to her. "I know I came on strong at first. I was overwhelmed at the ranch and feeling stretched to the max. Lately..." He seemed to consider for a moment, then forged ahead. "All the responsibility for Diamondback is on my shoulders, but Dad still pulls the strings and we're not seeing eye to eye. Today I had to go for a ride to blow off some steam."

"What happened between you?"

"He doesn't agree with putting in the biogas plant. I've showed him all the research. I've crunched the numbers. But he's dug in his heels and crossed his arms and said no."

Angela longed to reach out and touch his hand, but knew she didn't dare. "He's going through a difficult time. From what I gather, he was a vital workingman and now he's stuck inside and doing rehab."

"I know that. Seeing him this way is killing me, so arguing is making it all worse. My family's falling apart. Hell, I even called my cousin Ty to get his take on the whole thing."

"Ty?"

"Dad's nephew. Mom and Dad adopted him when he was a baby. He's a Diamond through and through. He reminded me that Dad is like a brick wall. There's just no easy way to break through."

"You'll figure it out," she assured him. "Diamondback means everything to both of you. It's natural that you're both very passionate about its direction."

"You're right. Diamondback—it's my life. I want to take it into the future, and Dad, he's just scared." He tilted his head and looked at her suspiciously. "Did you just go all social worker on me?"

She couldn't resist smiling just a little. "Of course not. You just needed to get it off your chest."

His hand rubbed absently over her foot, and he seemed completely unaware of the effect it was having on her. "Thanks for letting me vent. When I'm here, it's..."

"It's what?"

"Simpler. I can look at it with different eyes, and it makes sense. When I'm here I feel like even the smallest thing I do might make a difference to someone."

It did make a difference—to her. His words touched something inside her. She knew what it was like to need to act. She supposed that her feelings about her mother were similar to how Sam felt about his father. Beverly Beck would never leave her own personal hell and there was nothing Angela could say or do to change her mom's mind.

Sam had shared a part of himself with her today.

She didn't want to care; she didn't want to rely on someone only to be disappointed. And she was in grave danger of relying on—and caring for—Sam.

"What you do matters," she finally replied. "To your family. Your mother worships you, Sam."

"I know that. And I love Diamondback. I love the open space and I take pride in what we do. It's in my blood."

Of course it was. It only took seeing him in the saddle to know he was a rancher through and through. "But?"

"I don't know. I'm not satisfied. Maybe I need a constant challenge to keep me from being bored."

Was that all she was, then? Angela took her recently budded feelings and buried them again. She wasn't anyone's challenge. She knew she wasn't exciting and adventurous. Certainly not dynamic enough for him. He was all strength and energy and restless ambition.

"I guess Butterfly House is the lucky beneficiary of your boredom, then," she said carefully.

"Perhaps it is," he admitted. "Now, what are we going to do about tomorrow? What's left?"

Angela swallowed thickly. Maybe Sam was right. Maybe she did shut people out. Maybe there was a way to be friendly without divulging deeper secrets. Her confession that she'd been in a bad relationship had seemed to appease him. Angela felt her own sting of shame. How could she profess to be brilliant at her job when her own mother refused to leave her abuser every day?

Instead of talking about it, Angela chose to do the only thing she could—help the hundreds of other women looking to start again. Now, just as things were coming to fruition, she was forced to rely on Sam to get the job done. She didn't like the pattern that was forming, but she had no choice at this point.

"I need to run the vacuum over the floors."

"Consider it done."

"And organize all the food. There are a dozen teenagers who will need lunch, not to mention others dropping by."

And she had to start on that now. She knew how much food hungry teens could eat. There would be sandwiches but she'd planned on making sweets as well as a pot of homemade soup. She took her leg off Sam's lap—instantly missing the warmth of his body touching hers—and put her arms on the chair, pushing herself up. She took two steps and caught her breath. Maybe she could hobble around, but she couldn't stand on her feet for long and carrying anything was out of the question. Frustration simmered. Why now? Why couldn't this have happened next week?

Because she'd let Sam distract her and had suggested moving that silly box spring and mattress. It was her own fault, plain and simple.

"You need to keep that foot up."

"I need to get things ready."

"Do you ever accept help without fighting it every step of the way?"

She turned around, bracing her hand against the wall. "I'm not used to having help, to be honest. And when I do have it, it usually comes with conditions. Heck, you're only here because your support came with a seat on the board."

His eyes darkened. "Ouch."

It wasn't fair, not after all he'd just told her. "Sorry. I guess I'm not a very good patient."

He shrugged. "Maybe it was true, at first anyway. But I'm here now and I'm offering, string-free."

They were not in this together and she didn't want to feel as if they were. Her insides quivered. How many times had she wanted to stand side by side with her mother? To fight together? And each time she'd thought they were close to escaping, Beverly had backed down. Angela had ended up disappointed and alone. Not just alone—but with wounds that cut a little bit deeper. Feeling more and more alone and losing all faith and hope.

Sam was standing beside her now, but once this project was over he'd be gone. And she'd be standing alone again. So it came down to which was more important: Saving face or saving her feelings?

She already knew the answer. She was strong and resilient. She could withstand the loss of Sam Diamond. She couldn't lose Butterfly House, though. It had to succeed no matter what.

"I'll make you a list."

She hobbled to the kitchen and grabbed a notepad. Sitting at the table she began to write out what she needed. "I have the makings for sandwiches here and I can make those sitting down," she said, "but I need sweets. Cookies, brownies, and I was planning on making butter tarts. A few dozen muffins. And I was going to make a pot of soup in the slow cooker."

"That's it?" His brows lifted, studying the list over her shoulder. "That shouldn't be too much trouble. I don't know what you were making such a big fuss over."

The fuss was less over the items and more about needing his help once more. He was making himself indispensable and she didn't like it. Add into that the fact that she could still taste him on her lips and she needed to get him out of here as soon as possible.

She fought the urge to close her eyes. The warning bells pealed with a suffocating warning. Sam was taking over. Things with Steve had started the same way. He'd ingrained himself into her life until one day she woke up and realized he'd begun controlling it in a way she swore would never happen.

"I bought drinks but forgot cups." She wrote on the pad once more, trying to keep her hand from shaking. "And get paper ones, please, so we can recycle them."

"Leave it all to me. What about set up in the morning?"

"Clara, our first resident, is arriving first thing. She'll help me set up. But, Sam, really…"

"Sweets and soup. Consider it done." He ripped the list off the notepad and tucked it in his pocket.

She felt as though she was giving away control of the situation and it was killing her. This was her baby. If anything went wrong it was all on her. The trouble with it all was that she *wanted* to trust him. And that made her weak.

He put his hand on her shoulder and squeezed. "You don't believe me, do you?"

There was no accusation in the words. She turned her head and looked up at him. "It's not you, Sam. I don't really trust anyone."

"Maybe someday you'd care to share why that is." He said it quietly, a soft invitation. But she was already liking him too much. There could be no more kisses. No more shared intimacies. Definitely no sharing of dirty secrets.

"I doubt it," she answered truthfully. "But thank you. You're going above and beyond, and I do appreciate it." And after tomorrow she'd be able to breathe again.

"It's been known to happen once or twice. Once I commit to a thing, I give it one hundred percent. Don't worry about tomorrow. I promise."

He gave it one hundred percent, but, by his own admission, he got bored and moved on. That was what she had to remember.

"I'll be back in half an hour with the cups and some pain meds for that foot." He came back and took the pen from her hands, scribbling a number on the top. "If you need anything, that's my cell number."

"Got it."

"See you soon."

He left once more and Angela sat in the quiet. She touched her fingers to her lips.

She was usually so good at figuring people out from first impressions. She'd learned to read people. But the more she got to know Sam, the harder it was to reconcile him with the slick charmer who'd barged into their board meeting.

She closed her eyes. The worst of it all was that she had enjoyed being taken care of today. And that wasn't a good thing at all.

The rain Angela feared would ruin the day stayed well to the west, cushioned in the valleys of the Rockies. Instead, the summer day dawned clear and sunny with only a few cotton-ball clouds marring the perfect sky. She showered and hobbled to the kitchen to fix some tea and toast, waiting for Clara to arrive. She was due at nine, the teens at ten. For now there was little to do. True to his word, Sam had returned yesterday with a bottle of ibuprofen, paper cups and a willing hand as he gave the vacuum a turn around the downstairs. It was a leap of faith, but she was trusting him to deliver on the rest of his promises. So far he'd come good and it was either trust or blind panic. And she really didn't want to panic. She'd leave the hyperventilating for later when she had time for it.

At five to nine Clara arrived. Angela met her at the door. "Oh, you look wonderful," she exclaimed, standing back and examining Butterfly House's first official resident. It was really happening. After all this time, it was hard to believe. But seeing Clara on her doorstep with a suitcase made it real.

"I feel good," Clara admitted. Her brown hair fell in curls to her shoulders, and Angela noticed she'd put on some of the weight she'd lost during the first months she'd been in a shelter in Edmonton. She had lovely curves now, and dressed in denim capri pants and a loose blue shirt she looked casual and attractive. Angela wondered if the plain, slightly baggy style and understated color was intended to deflect attention. Trying to avoid being noticed— unconsciously or consciously—was common.

"Bring in your things, Clara. Three of the rooms

are ready and you can have your pick. Then we can set to work."

Clara brought in a suitcase and carryall. Angela held open the door but Clara immediately noticed her limp. "What did you do to yourself?"

"Dropped a box spring on my toe yesterday."

"You should have called. I would have come early to help."

Heat rose in Angela's cheeks. "I had some help, but thanks. And I'm certainly going to put you to work today. I don't think I'll be very effective herding teens."

Morris popped into the kitchen through the basement cat door and Clara put down her bags. "Well, hello there," she cooed, and a delighted Morris rubbed his head against her hand. "Aren't you handsome?"

"Be careful. He can be a biter."

"Don't be silly. What's your name, kitty?"

"Morris," Angela replied, watching with fascination. After the first incident with Sam, Morris had either hid out in the basement or simply stayed out of the way. He certainly didn't warm up to people as a rule. But here he was, snuggling up to Clara as if they were old friends. Perhaps her instinct about it being a man thing was dead-on.

"I'm glad you have a cat. Pets are so nonjudgmental. All they want is love."

Angela laughed. "Oh, I'm afraid Morris is typical cat. He judges on sight and has many demands. But it looks like you've passed the test. I'm glad. I rescued him and hoped he'd go over well here. I don't think I could bear to give him up now."

"He'll be great company. Now let's drop my things so we can get to work." Clara lifted her bags again and threw Angela a smile. Suddenly the day seemed full of possibilities.

They went upstairs and it was no surprise to Angela that Clara picked the sunny yellow room that matched her personality. Angela was glad that they'd finished it yesterday, and Clara could make the bed up with the new bedding later.

They'd just managed to set up the banquet table on the porch and put a tablecloth on it when Sam arrived. He lifted a hand from the steering wheel in greeting and Angela waved back, the now-familiar swirl of anticipation curling through her tummy. There was no doubt about it—she'd gone from dreading his appearance to looking forward to it. Something had changed yesterday and not just because of the kiss, but because they'd shared glimpses into their lives.

She resisted the urge to touch her hair, determined that any reaction she felt was kept inside and not broadcast for Sam or Clara to see.

He opened the back door of the truck cab and took out a plastic bin. "Someone call for food?"

"Morning," she said when he came closer. He

smiled. It was ridiculous that a smile should make her feel giddy, but it did. He'd come, just like he'd promised. She looked over to see if Clara was watching them, but she was busy putting drinks in a cooler on the porch. All in all, a sense of celebration and the feeling that everything was going to turn out all right was in the air.

"Good morning. How's the foot?"

"Sore," she admitted.

He lifted his hands a little. "Where do you want it?"

"Inside on the counter." She turned around and waved at Clara to come over. With the way she was feeling, a little interference would be a good thing. "Sam, this is Clara Ferguson. She's moving in today. Clara, Sam Diamond."

"Miss Ferguson." Sam put down the bin and held out his hand.

"Mr. Diamond."

Angela noticed the happy light dim in Clara's eyes for just a moment, and she didn't come forward to shake Sam's hand. Sam kept the smile on his face as he casually dropped the hand and looked at Angela.

"Sam's family is our biggest sponsor, Clara. His mother, Molly, sits on the board of directors. But his father's been ill, so in the meantime Sam has stepped in. He's been invaluable in getting the house ready for today."

As she said the words she knew they were true. Today couldn't have happened without him. She couldn't ever remember depending on someone so heavily. But she'd never taken on a project of this magnitude, either.

"It's an important project," Sam replied, and looked back at Clara again. "I hope you'll be happy here, Clara."

Clara lifted her chin. "I haven't been happy in a long time, Mr. Diamond. I'm looking forward to it."

Angela smiled at the fledgling confidence in Clara's voice. Yes, she'd do very nicely. Sam nodded at them both, picked up the bin and started up the porch steps. Angela followed at a slow hobble, wishing that Sam didn't look quite so good from the back view.

Sam was taking packages out of the bin when Angela arrived in the kitchen. He'd been unsure of what to say to Clara, especially when she seemed to withdraw into herself at his introduction. What should he have said? Was it better to address the issues plainly, or avoid the topic altogether? He was a rancher, no good at diplomacy, and today he was going to be put on the spot about Butterfly House. A few days ago he had considered today an annoying interruption in his schedule. But he felt differently now. He wanted to do and say the right thing. He wanted to be helpful. How could he when he couldn't even figure out the right way to speak to the women most affected by the project?

"Thank you, Sam, for bringing the food."

He put a tray of bakery muffins on the counter. "It was no trouble." He paused and turned to face her. "Delivering food is easy. But with Clara just now I didn't know what to say. I didn't want to say the wrong thing and offend her."

"You did fine," she replied, and the small half smile he was growing to look for tilted her lips. "You read the signs, which is good, and you didn't press her into shaking hands. It's a long process, Sam. When you've been abused, it stays with you forever. It's not surprising that she's not comfortable with close contact. Clara's come a long way and now she's ready to start over."

She sounded so logical, so professional. And perhaps a little bit distant. This was her element, he realized. She was more like her boardroom self today and he wasn't sure what to make of it. It was impressive, but he missed the flustered and slightly messed woman who huffed and puffed carrying furniture. Who sighed just a little when their lips touched. Whose lashes fluttered onto her cheeks when she opened up just a little about her past. Sam felt his heart constrict. How any man could treat a woman badly angered the hell out of him. "My mother would be better at this sort of thing."

Angela looked up at him. She looked so fresh and lovely in linen trousers and a cute white top—all airy and summery. Her glossy hair was pinned up today, and he missed the way the waves fell over her shoulders as they had yesterday when he'd leaned in and kissed her. His body tightened just thinking about it.

"Maybe she would, but maybe not. It might actually be better if it's you. Molly would have set an example for the women of Cadence Creek and that support system is crucial, it's true. But you could make a real difference, too. Over half the businesses in town are owned by men. Men who look up to you, and to your father. Men who might just have employment opportunities."

His hand paused on a bag of chocolate chip cookies. He thought back to the conversation he'd had with Angela in the Diamondback yard—that his presence was important here today for PR reasons. Was that all he was to her, then? It surprised him that the idea bothered him, when weeks ago he hadn't wanted anything to do with her—at all.

"Angela? The first of the kids are here." Clara's voice came through the screen door.

"I should get them organized," Angela said, and his annoyance grew. He wanted to gather her into his arms and kiss her again to see if her cool and collected demeanor was genuine or if he still had the ability to frazzle her. Right now, despite the limp, she seemed implacable.

"I'll bring in the rest of the things. Mom wanted to help so she sent a batch of her taco soup and insisted that store-bought brownies couldn't compare to her recipe." Indeed, Molly had seemed more than happy to take the time to cook for the event.

"Oh, how nice of her! I'll be right back to plate everything."

He watched her limp down the hall and frowned. Yesterday's kiss had done nothing less than fire something in him that he hadn't felt in a long time. And he discovered he was far from being done with it.

CHAPTER SEVEN

ANGELA ladled out soup to the line of kids, every now and then glancing up to watch Sam speak to the local Member of the Legislature. He looked so comfortable in the situation, his weight resting on one hip and his shoulders down and relaxed. She envied how easy he made it all look. The idea of being in the spotlight just about made her blood run cold. She was so much better behind the scenes. It had been Molly who had pushed for an open-house day. She'd been right—the foundation needed the exposure. But it definitely put Angela out of her comfort zone.

Sam had been so great today. First with providing the food she'd needed, and then hanging around to speak with people while she spent her time supervising and organizing, all at a snail's pace as she hobbled about on her sore foot. She handed over another soup bowl and Sam looked over and smiled, gave a little wave. She fluttered her fingers in response and then tucked a stray piece of hair behind her ear.

She knew very well she shouldn't be so happy he was here. It was the reaction of the moment, it wasn't real. Her future was with the foundation and her plans, not with Sam. It was just hard to remember that when he was around.

Sometimes she wondered what it would be like to truly be a part of someone's world, rather than a series of people simply passing through. What would it be like to be part of *his* world?

The very idea sent a curl of warmth through her, tempered by a touch of fear. It would be easy to lose herself in Sam. He was so charismatic, so dynamic. His outgoing personality would swallow her whole.

"Ms. Beck?" One of the kids said her name and drew her out of her thoughts. "Can I have more soup? It's good."

She shook the troubling thoughts away and smiled. "Sure you can." The teens had worked up an appetite and Clara had kept them in line throughout the morning, trimming dead branches off shrubs and clearing out the old flower gardens at the base of the porch. A local garden center had donated some bedding plants—the season was ending and it hadn't been difficult to convince them to part with their leftover stock. Now flats of brightly colored geraniums, marigolds and petunias waited to be planted. One more thing to make Butterfly

House home, to add some color and zip that was missing in so many of their lives.

She handed over the soup. "You've been a huge help. Thank you all for coming."

"It's been fun," one girl said, breaking off a piece of cookie. "I'd just be hanging around at home watching TV anyway."

The group of them belonged to an after-school club organized to keep local kids out of trouble. Now, in the summer months, they were left to their own devices more often than not. Giving them a project had been a good idea. Angela planned on speaking to the director again about partnering up. There was no reason why the two projects couldn't help each other.

"Yeah, me, too," said one of the boys. "Maybe we could take turns mowing the grass here or something. Whaddaya think, Ms. Beck?"

"I think it's a great idea. Tell you what. Come see me on Monday and we can set up a schedule."

"Cool."

She'd been so involved with talking to the group that she hadn't noticed Sam coming up the porch steps. "What plans are you concocting now?" he asked.

She wished she didn't get that jumped-up feeling every time she heard his voice. It didn't help that he was behind her and essentially blocking any escape off the veranda.

She began to lift her hands to her warm cheeks but stopped, dropping them to her sides. "The club is going to help out on a more regular basis. Isn't it great?"

"Sure it is." Sam smiled, but Angela sensed an awkwardness to his expression. He nodded briefly to the kids and then grabbed a paper plate.

His cool response seemed to have dimmed the enthusiasm, so Angela smiled broadly. "Hey, if someone is prepared to do my yardwork, I'll happily provide snacks." She grinned as sounds of approval came from the group. She looked at the lot of them. She knew their lives could be touched by a variety of problems—poverty, neglect, alcoholism—providing some home cooking was the least she could do. For some of them it might be the best meal they got all day.

"And have you taken time to eat anything?" Sam gave her elbow a nudge. "You haven't stopped all morning. A bird can't fly on one wing, you know."

His intimate smile was disarming and rattled her further. He'd noticed her movements even though they'd been doing different things. And his words weren't critical. Instead they felt caring. "Not yet," she replied, realizing her tummy was feeling a little hollow. "You?"

"Nope. And Mom's taco soup is one of my favorites. Let's get some before this crowd drains the pot."

While Angela got their soup, Sam loaded his plate with a ham sandwich, a handful of potato chips and a selection of raw veggies. He led her away from the teens to a quieter spot on the porch steps. "What?" he asked, as they sat balancing the food on their knees. "I'm a growing boy."

She snorted. "Sam, if you grow any bigger you'll be..."

"Be what?"

She stared into her bowl. Even what was intended as easy banter flustered her beyond belief. She struggled to find a word and grabbed on to one she'd heard the kids use this morning. "Ginormous."

He chuckled. "You haven't met my father, have you?"

"No."

"My mom always said he was as big as a barn door." The warmth dropped out of his voice a little, replaced with sadness. "He's not as big as he used to be."

She wished she could say something to make it better, but she knew that there were times that words simply couldn't fix what was wrong. There was no other comfort she could give other than a paltry "I'm sorry, Sam. It must be so hard for all of you."

"Yes, it is. After yesterday...I talked to my mom.

I think she's finally starting to realize she needs help."

Angela felt guilt slide down her spine. "I never meant that she should have to cook for today," she said quietly. "I know she has enough on her plate looking after your father." Sam had pushed and made it impossible for her to say no. If she'd known he was going to go home and foist it on Molly, she would have insisted on doing it herself. "Please thank her for me, will you? If I'd known that was your plan, I would have made a different suggestion."

"She wanted to," Sam replied easily. "She's been so wrapped up in Dad's recovery that it was good for her to focus on something else—something positive. I was going to go out and buy everything and she insisted she help. So don't feel the least bit bad, Angela. You were right. It's more meaningful when people put themselves into a project rather than just 'throwing money at it,' as you said."

She stared at her toes. Oh, how she wished she'd never said those words! "I'm sorry I said that to you," she replied quietly, putting down her empty bowl. He held out his plate, and she took a chip from it. "Thanks."

"No, you were right to. I've been like Mom. So absorbed in the issues at Diamondback that I couldn't see anything else. There are other things—

important things—going on. I've enjoyed helping the last few weeks. I care about…"

Hope seemed to hover in the middle of her chest. After their first disastrous meeting she'd wanted him to appreciate what Butterfly House meant. That was *all* she wanted, she reminded herself. "You care about what?"

He popped a chip in his mouth, chewed and swallowed. "I care what happens to this place and feel invested in its success. That's new for me."

"I'm glad." And she was. The sinking feeling in the pit of her stomach was inconsequential. There was not a single reason why she should be feeling disappointed.

"That's what I told our MLA, and the reporter from the paper, too. That we as a community need to get involved."

Angela looked over at him. He was still wearing his Stetson and the way it shaded his face made him look mysterious and delicious. He was so different from anyone she'd ever known. No matter how confusing her feelings were regarding him, she was, for the moment, glad that Molly had stepped away from the board and Sam had taken her place. If he meant what he said, she'd managed to bring Sam around after that horrible first meeting when he'd been so dismissive. She remembered thinking if she could accomplish that, she could accomplish anything. Today was a victory in every sense of the word. But it felt hollow somehow.

"Thank you," she whispered. "For getting it. For helping."

"You're welcome."

There was a finality to the word that was a let-down. It occurred to her that after today she'd hardly need him around. Clara was here now and could help with the final touches to the house. The yard work was done. By the first of August, a few more beds would be occupied. Angela would be filling her days with the day-to-day management of the house and liaising with support programs. Sam would be back at Diamondback, overseeing the ranch and the new facility he was planning. It was as it should be. The sooner things got back to normal the sooner she could stop having all these confusing feelings. Sam Diamond was a distraction she didn't need.

But even as she knew deep down it was for the best, she was going to miss the anticipation of seeing him walk through the front door and hearing his voice challenge her.

"I'd better get back. I should make another pot of coffee and get those kids going again."

"They working out all right?"

She met his gaze. "Sure, why wouldn't they?" She realized he'd worn the same awkward expression when talking about Clara this morning. "Is there something wrong with having them here?"

He shook his head. "Of course not. I'm just not used to any of this. I don't know how to talk to people who…"

"Who weren't brought up by Molly and Virgil Diamond?"

He looked so earnest that her heart gave a little thump. "Maybe," he replied honestly. "I had a sheltered life, I guess, with advantages. I don't know what to say to people. You have a way that I don't, Angela. I admire that."

She was shocked. "But you handled the people part so well today—you looked totally at ease!"

He chuckled. "That's different. It's… Aw, heck. It's easier to put on an act when it's something official. But you—you're genuine. That's special."

Her? Special? He had no idea how much easier it had been to deal with troubled teens than face the press. "You played to your strengths today, Sam, and I appreciate it. As far as the kids go—they're just kids. There's no secret code. They just want to feel visible, important to someone."

She looked up and saw Clara waving her over. The photographer from the paper was standing close by and Clara's face looked absolutely panicked.

"There's something wrong with Clara, will you excuse me?"

Clara's eyes filled with relief when she arrived.

"Oh, good. I was trying to explain that I don't want my picture taken," Clara said to Angela in a low voice.

"Of course," Angela assured her. The last thing residents needed was their faces plastered over the media. "Why don't you get some lunch? I'll take it from here."

She spoke briefly to the photographer, who was undeterred. He wanted a picture for the paper to go with the story. Angela's insides froze when she thought about standing before a camera lens. After a few moments of strained diplomacy, she heard Sam's voice at her back.

"Anything I can help with?"

Sam was close by her shoulder and she looked up at him. "The photographer wants a picture for the paper."

"So what's the problem?"

"I don't do pictures, Sam."

Sam's brow puckered. "Will you excuse us a moment?" he asked the photographer pleasantly. Then, with a light hand at her back, he led her aside.

"You don't enjoy having your picture taken?"

If he only knew. She was so much better in the background. It was why she had wanted to be a director but not the face of the foundation. "It can be a fine line between starting over and trying to keep under the radar, you know? Worse for Clara. But I don't do photos. I just don't."

"Is that reasonable? You're the director here."

But the reasons went bone deep. There was the privacy thing, and perhaps she should be past it by now. But there was that horrible slap she hadn't expected, the one that had snapped her head around so quickly she'd dropped to her knees.

Steve had taken a picture of her and waved it in her face. She recognized the young woman in the photo all too well and she hated that person. "A reminder so you don't step out of line again," he'd said, taking a magnet and sticking it on the fridge. She hadn't posed for a photograph since.

She shuddered at the memory. "You do it," she suggested.

"But you're the director," Sam argued. "This is your baby. You should be in the picture."

Her throat constricted. "I can't," she whispered, her voice raw. That would make her public. It would make her feel…exposed. And she had no idea how to explain it without breaking down.

Silence spun out for several long seconds. Sam's gaze never left her face and she blinked rapidly. Then he put his hand on her shoulder, warm and strong. "Then let's do it together. We can both be in it."

As compromises went it was a good one. "I don't know."

"At some point you need to step out of the shadows, sweetheart. Otherwise he's still winning."

Sam was right. Nothing would sidetrack her from making this a success—not even her own fears. She was depending on Butterfly House to set the bar. A brilliant track record would follow her when she went to set up similar houses in other towns, maybe even other provinces. Maybe one day the one person she hoped would need help most would take that step. If her mother ever wanted to break free, a place like Butterfly House should be waiting for her.

"We just need to show a unified front for a few minutes. A couple of snaps and we're done."

A couple of snaps that would put her face in print. Angela wondered what Sam would think if he knew the real truth. She'd made it sound so *over* when they'd spoken earlier in the week. But beneath the businesslike social worker there was a victim still struggling to overcome her own issues. She was a complete fraud and terrified of being found out.

So today she would stop acting like a victim. "Okay," she agreed, feeling slightly nauseous but glad Sam was there beside her. "Let's do it and get it over with."

The photographer stepped in. "Are you ready?"

"Oh, yes. Sure." Angela pasted on a brittle meet-the-press smile. "This is Sam Diamond, one of our board members. He'll be in the photo with me."

"Mr. Diamond, of course. Thanks for sparing the time. Let's make it a nice casual shot, shall we? Maybe you can sit on the picnic table here, with Miss Beck beside you? That way the height discrepancy is minimized."

Sam shrugged and perched on the edge of the wood table.

"Right. Put your foot there, perhaps?"

Sam put his left foot on the bench seat of the table, while his right leg balanced on the ground. All it did was emphasize the long length of his legs.

"Now, Miss Beck, if you'll move in closer and stand beside him…"

Butterflies dipped and swirled and she fought to keep the professional smile glued to her lips. She moved closer to Sam until she was standing beside him. But not touching. Sitting beside him on the step during lunch had been close enough.

The photographer looked through his lens and then lowered his camera again. "Not quite right. If you could slide in a little, please. Maybe put your hand on Mr. Diamond's shoulder, Miss Beck."

Touch him? In a personal way? For a photo? Angela was suddenly at a loss as to how to express the inappropriateness of it without sounding offensive. This whole thing was growing more uncomfortable by the second. She scrambled to come up with an alternative. "What if I stand a little behind him, like this?" She moved in behind his shoulder and instead of placing her hand on his shoulder, placed it on the top of the table instead. The bulk of Sam's body hid her from the camera lens which suited her just fine. There was no doubt in her mind that he'd be the focal point of the picture.

"That's good," he replied, lifting the camera again.

She wasn't touching Sam but their bodies were close enough that it felt warm and intimate. His morning exertions had magnified the scent of his aftershave. It filled her nostrils, the clean, masculine scent making her mouth water.

She wanted to touch him. That was the heck of it.

"One more," the photographer said. "The Butterfly House team," he chattered on. Sam turned his head and looked up at her briefly.

"A team," he said, a grin lighting his face. "Imagine that."

His smile warmed her all over and she began to relax. "Pretty impossible if you ask me. You did drop a bed on my foot."

"You dropped that yourself, but nice try."

It really wasn't so bad after all, she realized. Sam's easy posture relaxed her as well. "Turn around and pay attention," she scolded.

He dutifully turned around. Angela couldn't hold

in the little snort that bubbled up at his sudden obedience.

"All done. Thank you both." The photographer lowered his camera and smiled.

"That's it?" She looked up in surprise. It had been painless after all! She'd nearly forgotten that there was anyone behind the camera.

"That's it," he confirmed.

Sam's teasing had made Angela forget the awkwardness of being so close to him, but it came back tenfold when Sam leaned back against her for just a moment, his shoulder pressed lightly up against her breastbone. It was an odd moment where she suddenly felt very much like a part of a team, and something more. Intimacy. There was awareness, but there was also an increasing level of comfort with the way his body fitted against hers or the way his skin felt when they came in contact with each other. She'd never really experienced that kind of intimacy before and she wasn't sure what to do with it. She surely didn't want it—even if it did feel nice.

"Thanks for this," she murmured.

"My pleasure," Sam said, seemingly unaware of the turmoil he created within her. "Don't work too hard, now."

Hard work was just what she needed to forget about Sam—and her confusing feelings.

* * *

The flowers nodded their bright heads, perhaps a little unevenly but cheerfully nonetheless. The mess from the buffet lunch was tidied and Clara and Angela were packaging up the leftovers in the kitchen. The house was strangely silent after the commotion, and when Angela heard a distinct meowing, she went to the cat door and unlocked the flap. "It's safe now," she said soothingly as Morris stuck his orange head through the hole.

She'd locked him downstairs with full bowls of food and water shortly before Sam's arrival, knowing he'd hide in his basket anyway during the ruckus of people running in and out all day. She'd also worried about doors being left open in the chaos and him getting out. When Morris was out, he was a terror to try to get back. And the longer he was with her, the more Angela couldn't bear the thought of parting with him. He'd been her company on long nights. He never judged. He just did his thing and came for a cuddle when it suited him. Angela understood it perfectly.

Clara looked out the kitchen window and gave a little sigh. "Well, there's a sight."

Angela went to the window and looked out. Sam was working on the old woodpile that had been created when the previous owners had cut down a birch in the backyard. He'd taken off his cotton shirt and now wore a plain white T-shirt and jeans. Beside him were two of the boys from today's group, stacking the cut wood in even piles. One of them said something and Sam laughed, tipping back his head. For a guy who was so awkward around the teens, he was fitting in incredibly well.

"He likes you," Clara said quietly. "I can tell. It's in the way he looks at you."

"I'm not interested," Angela replied, turning away from the sight. But it was too late. She already had the picture of him in her mind, blended with the leftover reactions from their picture-taking episode. Sam was persistent, she'd give him that. And he'd seen the day through, which was great. But it was time he went on his way. It was time to take the next step—the day-to-day running of the house. The last thing she needed was Sam underfoot and distracting her with his slow swagger and sexy smile.

"Yes, you are," Clara contradicted. "What you are is scared."

Angela looked at Clara. The other woman's pleasant smile was gone. Instead she looked worried—and sympathetic. Clara seemed to understand things a little too well. And while she wanted to be friends with the women here, that couldn't extend to examining her own problems.

Angela forced herself to smile. "Which one of us is the social worker?"

Clara's shoulders relaxed and she resumed packing vegetables into a plastic container. "You know the saying about walking in someone else's shoes?"

"Sure."

"You've walked in mine. There's a big difference between appreciating how a man looks and acting on it. There's an even bigger gap between wanting it all and being brave enough to go after it."

Amen, Angela thought. Clara put it all so succinctly, summarizing the quandary in a way that Angela hadn't been able to because her emotions had gotten in the way. For the first time Angela admitted to herself that she had been flirting with other dreams. Dreams in which she had a perfectly normal happily ever after. But Clara was right. It was not the same as taking the bull by the horns and going after it. She wasn't even sure it existed in real life. She picked up a platter and opened a bottom cupboard, hiding her face from Clara. "I guess neither of us are there yet."

Clara shook her head. "I know I'm not. It's too soon. But what's stopping you, Angela? How long…" She paused. "Forget I asked that. It's not my business."

"I'm happy as I am. I made my choices and I don't regret a one." She grinned, determined to change the subject. "And now you're here. This is what I've been working toward all along. So don't worry about me. I'm exactly where I want to be."

Angela looked out the window as she passed by

to the fridge. Sam was shrugging his shirt back on and she watched the play of the muscles in his shoulders. He shook the boys' hands before sending them on their way. Clara was right. She was scared. Of Sam. Of her feelings which seemed to grow stronger every day. Of everything. This job was the only place where she felt she had absolute control and confidence and that was how it was going to stay. She couldn't be rational about Sam, and she had to be. Her life depended on seeing things clearly.

Sam knocked on the back door and Clara let him in. "Do you ladies need anything else?" he asked.

Angela put Molly's slow cooker back in the bin. "No, I think we're good. We've washed up Molly's dishes and they're all here for her. Please thank her, Sam. Everything was delicious."

"Thank her yourself. She told me to ask you to dinner when things were through."

He had left his shirt unbuttoned and the tails hung around the hips of his jeans. Angela didn't know how to answer. An invitation to Diamond-back! That hadn't happened before, even when Molly had worked with her on the project.

But it was different somehow. This felt personal, and it was crossing a line. Especially on the heels of Clara's observation. As much as Angela was tempted to accept, she knew she couldn't. "I'm sorry, but I can't. We need to get Clara settled and everything."

"Clara, you're welcome to come, too. It's just a barbecue on the deck. You both deserve a break after today. Surely you have all day tomorrow to get settled?"

Silence fell on the kitchen as Clara looked at Angela and Angela looked at Sam. He was making it awfully hard to say no. The idea of a dinner full of conversation and laughter—Molly and Sam both had such an easy way about them—was hard to resist. When was the last time she'd sat around a table with friends enjoying a meal? Relaxing? And she'd just determined that it was a good thing that they'd barely see each other after today. He was really hitting her in a vulnerable spot.

"It would mean a lot. Mom feels badly for leaving you in the lurch and not helping more. And it would cheer her up to have people around. You know my mother, Angela." His dark eyes pleaded with her. "She is usually so outgoing, but she hardly leaves the house nowadays. It's so rare that she looks forward to anything. Surely you can spare an hour or two?"

Angela was still debating when Morris stalked in from the living room and halted a few feet from Sam as if to say *hey, what's he doing here?*"

Then, to Angela's great surprise, he came forward and rubbed on Sam's pant leg. Sam knelt down and stroked between Morris's ears. Angela could hear the purrs clear across the kitchen.

"Looks like your cat's had a change of heart," he said. He stopped rubbing and instantly Morris leaned against his hand, looking for more. For a moment Angela was transported back to yesterday, and the way Sam's hand had felt on her ankle, warm and reassuring. The way his lips had rubbed against hers. She couldn't blame Morris for wanting more—even if it did make him a bit of a traitor.

"So what do you say about dinner? If we had company, I think Mom would bring Dad outside to eat with us. He could use the change of scenery."

It was the mention of his father that tipped the balance. She knew Sam was struggling with the changes happening in his family and especially with his relationship with his father. She'd be small and insecure if she let a few misgivings keep a sick man from an enjoyable evening. "Oh, all right," she relented. It's not like it was just the two of them. There'd be other people around. Goodness, she'd hardly have to speak to Sam if she didn't want to. She could catch up with Molly, after all. She'd missed Molly, who'd been such a blessing during the early stages of the project. "We'll finish here and meet you at the ranch."

"Great."

He gave Morris one last pat and stood. "I'll take

that with me." He held out his hands for the bin.
Angela picked it up and placed it in his hands, careful not to touch him in any way. The earlier resolve
stood. Dinner changed nothing.

"Tell Molly not to go to any fuss," she said, looking up at him.

"It'll just be casual, don't worry. See you in an
hour or so."

She saw him to the door and watched him drive
away until the sound of his truck engine faded.
She sighed, wondering how on earth this had happened, and the bigger question: What on earth was
she going to wear?

CHAPTER EIGHT

FOR an hour Sam wondered if Angela was truly going to show up. It was nearly six o'clock and he'd had a fresh shower and changed clothes, helped move Virgil out onto the deck overlooking the valley, and now he turned the chicken over in the marinade even though it was already evenly coated.

He wrinkled his brow. Little things about Angela didn't add up in the usual way, and he wondered if there was more to the story than she was telling him. If? He was sure there must be. Nothing could be as cut-and-dried as she'd made in sound in a few short sentences.

Her lips were soft and sweet when he'd kissed her, but she'd pulled away first. She was fiercely dedicated to the project but panicked when it came to being the center of attention. She bantered easily with the teenagers but froze when it came to the press. And most miraculous of all—she'd managed to get him talking about himself. And yet she'd always kept the topic of conversation away from herself, only revealing what he suspected was the bare minimum.

All in all it made him wonder how best to proceed. The last thing he wanted to do was frighten her or come across as intimidating. He wasn't sure if a casual touch to him was equally casual to her. All in all, being involved with Angela in any way was a bit like walking through a minefield, not wanting to make a single misstep lest everything blow up in his face.

He was beginning to think he was in big trouble.

"Muss be sommme girrrl."

Sam looked over at his father. Virgil's speech was getting better but he still had trouble enunciating clearly, and often his words were drawn out. There was no mistaking the sparkle in his eyes, though, or the grin on his face—even if it was lopsided because of the lingering paralysis. It felt good to have the old, easy teasing between them again.

"I'm hungry, that's all."

The rusty laugh that came from Virgil warmed Sam's heart. It had been too long since he had heard his father laugh. Too long since they'd had a conversation without arguing, or lately, because of the speech difficulty, without disapproving grunts. "Uh-huh," Virgil replied.

"I know. Can't kid a kidder, right?"

A gleam of approval lit Virgil's eyes. Sam hadn't brought a girl home for a family dinner for years.

If Angela knew what his parents had to be thinking, she'd be halfway to Edmonton by now. Sam had to tread carefully. "This isn't a date, so go easy on her, Dad. She's skittish."

"Like yrrr motherrr."

"Mom?"

Virgil nodded. "Shy when we met. Hard work."

Sam chuckled, then sobered. Without knowing the full details of Angela's past, Sam knew something terrible had shaped who she'd become. It was more than shyness.

In the end he wanted what his parents had. Virgil's illness had not only affected Sam's parents but Sam himself. Suddenly he was very aware of mortality. Molly and Virgil wouldn't be around forever. It wasn't just the responsibility of Diamondback that Sam worried about. It was the legacy. Things couldn't go on, fractured the way they were, with all the arguing and with Ty wandering all over the continent. Family needed to stick together. And it was Angela who'd shown him that.

"You warm enough, Dad?" He changed the subject, not wanting to delve into things any deeper. He hated that his father had to sit in a wheelchair. Physio was working with him with a walker, but he could only use it under supervision and for short periods of time. He looked so frail, unable to get up and take charge in his usual good-natured, blustery way. The stroke had altered Virgil in so many ways. He was short-tempered and while Virgil had always been stubborn, he'd also been open-minded. Not now. Sam was pretty sure that fear was making the old man hold on too tight.

"Isss thirrrty degrees. Fine."

The annoyance was back in Virgil's voice and Sam backed off, not wanting to cause any trouble when guests were expected. "Okay, okay."

A car door slammed, followed by another. His heart gave a leap.

He tested the grill and found the temperature just right and when Molly brought the ladies back through the French doors, he was busy putting chicken breasts on the grates.

"Virgil, this is Angela Beck and Clara Ferguson." Molly made the introductions as Sam turned around.

Angela had changed her clothes. Sam's mouth went dry looking at her. She was pretty as a picture in a floral linen skirt and a cotton sweater the color of the prairie sky as the sun came up. She kept her hair off her face with a simple cream headband, the dark waves of it falling gracefully to her shoulders. She looked so young and fresh it made him feel all of his thirty-seven years. And yet the nerves that centered in his belly made him feel like a teenager again. He'd never met anyone who could make him feel that way before.

Perhaps having her over for a family dinner was

a mistake. He was afraid he was going to be horribly transparent, gawking at her the way he was right now.

Molly's speculative gaze lit on him and he went back to the barbecue, shutting the lid. Yes, a family dinner probably wasn't the smartest move. Molly had been pushing him for grandkids for years and would read more into it than it was. Sam knew Angela well enough by now to know that she could easily be chased away by well-meaning innuendoes. She reminded him of a skittish colt who needed a gentle and strong hand. He should have asked her out somewhere private. But where would that be in Cadence Creek? There was only the Wagon Wheel Diner and tongues would set to wagging the moment they walked in the door. She'd hate gossip. As would he.

"Mr. Diamond, it's so good to meet you. Thanks for inviting us to your home."

Sam schooled his features and stepped away from the grill in time to see Angela take Virgil's hand in hers and squeeze. Sam saw his father's eyes light up and she smiled. "Oh, goodness," she teased, "now I see where Sam got that wicked grin."

"Chip offf old block." His sideways smile was back. Angela laughed in response and Sam saw a touch of color bloom in her cheeks.

"Hmmm," she replied, raising a knowing eyebrow. "I see I'm going to have to watch out for you."

Sam's heart turned over at the happy expression on Virgil's face. She couldn't possibly know how much this one moment meant to his father— or to him. He'd watched over the weeks as his father's dignity—his manhood and vitality—had been stripped away. He'd been helpless to change it, and had made it worse at times with their arguments over ways to make the ranch more environmentally friendly. With one smile and a few words Angela had given something back to Virgil. Did she have any idea how well she fitted here without even trying?

Sam put his hand on the deck railing. He was a fool. He kept telling himself that he was doing it for his mother, or that he was after friendship, but there came a time when a man couldn't lie to himself any longer. He was in the precarious position of falling for Angela Beck completely. All it would take was the slightest push and he'd be over the edge. The most shocking thing of all was that he almost welcomed the leap.

"Mr. Diamond, this is my friend Clara. She's the first resident at Butterfly House."

"Thank you for making me feel so welcome here," Clara said. She didn't move to take Virgil's hand, and Sam remembered what Angela had said about close contact. Sympathy for her mixed with respect for what Angela was doing. Whatever had happened in the past, Clara was getting a fresh start in Cadence Creek. Angela met his gaze and gave him a sweet smile. He knew it was a thank-you for including Clara in the evening. But for Sam, the smile meant more. It tethered them together as architects of something good. Angela was the driving force, but Sam had long stopped begrudging the time spent away from Diamondback. Somewhere along the way he'd started believing. In the foundation. In *her*.

"What do you do, Clara? What sort of job will you be looking for?" Molly spoke up.

Clara looked over at Molly, who was laying out napkins on a glass-topped table. "I'm a licensed practical nurse," she replied. "I'm hoping to find a job close by, maybe at a nursing home or clinic. I'm not sure how long my car can withstand a long commute, but right now anything would be wonderful."

"I see," Molly replied. Sam stared at Clara. She could be the answer to his prayers. He'd been after Molly to hire some help with Virgil and Clara would be perfect.

But Molly would take convincing, and he needed to speak to her as well as Angela before any offer was made. Surely Angela would be pleased?

"And what do you have cooking there?" Angela left Molly and Clara chatting and came closer to the barbecue as he opened the lid and grabbed a pair of tongs to flip the chicken. She was still limping but not as badly as she had earlier in the day. She even smelled good, like outdoors and the soft lily of the valley that grew in the shade of Molly's weeping birch grove. He tamped down the wave of desire that flared and focused on brushing the meat with leftover marinade. "Mom's Greek chicken."

"It looks delicious," she replied lightly.

He looked down at her, staring at the top of her head. "You're late. You weren't going to come, were you?"

She shrugged, but still didn't meet his eye. "I thought twice about it."

"But here you are. And looking mighty pretty." He couldn't resist the compliment. Besides, he knew it would make her look at him, and she did. Her blue-green eyes met his and he felt the alarms go off all over again. Falling for her would be so easy. He should put an end to it right now. It hadn't been difficult in the past. The attraction he was feeling now was simply physical and would go away in time, wouldn't it?

The difference was that he wasn't willing to explore that attraction with her as he had been with other woman. She wasn't the sort of girl a man could be casual with. And so he looked away and absently flipped the chicken even though it didn't need flipping.

"I came because I thought it would be good for Clara to meet a few more people. Especially people who are supportive and not prone to judge."

"That's the only reason?"

She lifted her chin. "Should there be another one?"

It was his turn to shrug as he closed the lid on the grill again. "Not necessarily."

"Molly invited me. Isn't that enough?"

He didn't answer. Molly hadn't invited her at all. It had been Sam's suggestion. At his continued silence she grabbed his arm. "Sam, tell me you didn't foist us on your mother after all she did to help today?"

"She said it was a great idea." Those hadn't been her precise words, but the meaning was the same.

"What do you want from me, Sam?" She lowered her voice so that it was barely a murmur at his side.

He couldn't help it; his gaze dropped to her lips. They were full and a slight sheen of gloss made them look soft and supple.

"I don't want anything," he replied quietly. "I'm playing it by ear here, same as you. Maybe I just wanted to see you away from Butterfly House and get to know you better. Isn't that what friends do?"

There, well done. He'd played the friends card. That would help dial things back a notch. It was bad enough he was looking at her lips as if they were coated in sugar and he had a sweet tooth. She didn't need to be getting any notions of her own.

Her eyes cooled and her lips formed a thin line. "Butterfly House makes me tick. And that's probably all you need to know."

She turned away and went to join Molly and Clara who were setting the table. Sam caught his father's gaze and felt a flash of kinship as Virgil gave him a familiar look that said *you've got your work cut out for you with that one.*

As the meat sizzled on the grill, he watched Angela work her magic. The three women talked as they worked and the tired tension around Molly's mouth seemed to evaporate as her smile became more relaxed. Angela had a way about her that put everyone at ease, he realized, and she did it all effortlessly. She'd worked that skill on him, too, getting him talking when normally he held his problems close to his chest. There was a burst of laughter and Sam watched as Molly put her hand along Angela's back, a kind of pseudo-hug that spoke of comfort and affection. Angela's dark head was next to his mother's gray-streaked one, and a sense of certainty struck Sam right in his core.

Through the years he'd spent time on unsatisfying relationships without knowing why. Now it made sense. None of those other women could measure up to Molly. None of them had her grace, wisdom or strength. She'd led by example and set the bar high—a standard no one had been able to meet.

But Angela did. And the hell of it was she wanted nothing to do with what he had to offer.

The sun started its slow descent as they lingered over dinner. Angela couldn't remember a time when she'd felt this relaxed and hyped up all at once. There was something different here tonight. She was so used to being an outsider but tonight she had been welcomed and more importantly— she'd actively *accepted* the welcome. She'd opened her heart, just a crack, to the Diamond family. How could she help it? Her heart had gone out to Virgil the moment he'd teased her and his smile had shown her what Sam's would look like in thirty years. Still charming. Still powerful. It had grabbed her and had yet to let go. A lump formed in her throat as she watched Molly cut Virgil's chicken into tiny pieces because managing two utensils proved beyond his abilities. When she finished she patted her hand and the look they shared spoke of so much love it made Angela want to weep.

It was hard to believe such trust and devotion existed but she had living proof tonight. It was rare. She knew that well enough. It would be easy to believe herself a part of it, but she wasn't. She was on the fringes, always the outsider looking in and wishing. For a moment she was angry with Sam. Didn't he realize how much he had here? How lucky he was? And he was determined to argue with his father over it. Molly and Virgil had given him everything a son could want while she'd been hiding in her clumsily mended secondhand clothes, scrimping and saving so that she could one day simply get out and choose her own life.

All the fluttery feelings she got when Sam was around couldn't disguise the truth. They were from different worlds and wanted different things. She should never have come tonight. It only made her wish for things that she would never have.

"Penny for your thoughts." Sam was seated across from her and his low voice sent shivers of pleasure along her skin.

"They're lovely, aren't they?" she replied, nodding at his parents and then meeting his gaze. Sam's dark eyes were watching her steadily and it made her pulse start knocking around like crazy.

"They've been there for each other as long as I can remember," Sam murmured. He glanced over at his parents holding hands while they chatted with Clara. "Even when my cousin came to live with us, there was no question or debate. Mom wanted to adopt him and Dad said yes without blinking an eye—even though Ty was a handful."

"Where's Ty now?"

"Here and there." Sam frowned. "He and Dad

didn't see eye to eye and Ty rebelled by becoming a rodeo star." Sam gave a half smile. "He loves it but considers it a perk that it drives Dad crazy." The smile faltered. "He hasn't been back since Dad's stroke, either. I think it's bothered Dad more than he wants to admit. Especially since we've been at odds more and more often over the biogas thing."

"Why can't you let it go, Sam?" Surely it wasn't worth destroying their relationship.

His gaze never flinched. "Because I'm right. Because sustainability is important. And because he knows it and doesn't want to admit it. It isn't really about the development. It's about him, and how he's dealing with things changing. I'm trying to be patient, but I'm not doing a very good job."

She chuckled. "I confess I'm a bit relieved."

"Relieved?" He paused with his fork in midair.

"Your family was looking rather perfect, Sam, with a complete lack of dysfunction. It's quite intimidating for a social worker."

"Nothing to fix?"

She couldn't help but laugh at his wry expression. "Something like that."

He smiled. "You've already helped, did you know that?"

She felt her cheeks heat and she dropped her eyes to her plate, but his encouraging words warmed her during the rest of the meal.

Virgil tired as they sipped tea; Molly enlisted

Sam's help to get him to bed while Clara and Angela insisted on clearing the table. Angela couldn't help but marvel at the state-of-the-art appliances, the solid pine cupboards and soaring ceilings. It was a stark contrast to the dingy kitchen Angela and her mother had kept in Edmonton, where the winter drafts froze up the kitchen window and nothing ever quite gleamed. She'd dreamed of having a place like this someday, dreamed of sharing it with her mother; the two of them living in peace. The shelters she had planned would never be this grand, relying as they did on donations and general goodwill. And her mother would never come, would she?

And yet Angela stared at the wealth around her and knew she couldn't stop trying; it was just like Sam felt about Diamondback. To give up Butterfly House would mean giving up on her mom. And giving up would break her heart.

She was aware of Sam returning but he went out on to the deck as Molly joined them at the sink.

"Oh, thank you, girls. My goodness, you've got it all cleaned up."

"The least we could do after such a great meal, Mrs. Diamond." Clara folded her dishcloth.

"You call me Molly. Everyone else does."

"Molly." Clara hung the dishcloth over the faucet. "I noticed the quilt on the back of your sofa. It's beautiful."

"Do you sew, Clara?"

"I used to. I like doing things with my hands."

"I've got another one on the frames in one of the spare rooms if you'd like to see it. A wedding-ring pattern in wine and cream."

"That would be wonderful."

Molly looked over at Angela, but for once Angela was unable to read the older woman's eyes. "I think Sam wants to speak to you about something, Angela."

"Oh, are you sure?" There was something about being alone in the twilight with Sam that made her hesitate.

"You go ahead," Molly replied. "I'll look after Clara."

How could she refuse without looking desperate or like a coward?

She paused at the French doors, gathering her courage. She could do this. His commitment to Butterfly House was over and so she just needed to reset the boundaries. They could redefine their relationship. If it even was a relationship—it was really more of an acquaintance, wasn't it?

She stepped outside and held her breath.

Sam stood at the top of the steps leading down to the garden. His arms were spread, his hands on the rail posts and she watched, transfixed, as he stretched, the pose highlighting the lean muscle that made up his body.

For the first time in years, Angela felt the ground shift beneath her feet. After focusing on her career, on the lives of others for so long, she wanted something for herself. And what she wanted—*who* she wanted—was Sam. It didn't matter about the justifications or reasons or differences in their lives. Nothing stopped the wanting. The only thing holding her back was that it scared her out of her wits. She wanted to believe in him so badly it terrified her.

"Sam?"

He turned. "You came. I wasn't sure you would."

Her pulse hammered in her wrists, her throat. "Why?"

"You avoided me all night."

Her voice came out at a whisper. "I wish you didn't always have to be so honest."

"I don't make it easy for you, do I?"

She shook her head. An owl hooted in the distance, a soulful cry that echoed through the garden. The sweet summer scent of Molly's rosebushes filled the air. Somewhere in a pasture to the right, a couple of cows lowed mournfully. This was Sam's world. And for tonight she'd gotten a taste of it. A bittersweet taste.

"Let me make it easier." He held out his hand. "Come for a walk with me."

She hesitated, but he waited, holding out his hand. Finally she took it, loving the feel of his warm fingers encircling hers. She followed him down the steps one at a time, only feeling a twinge of pain in her toe when she put all her weight on it. She expected him to let her hand go once they reached the bottom. But he didn't. He kept it firmly in his grasp as they wandered through the garden with slow steps.

"You didn't mention Clara was a licensed practical nurse," he finally said, halting and turning to face her.

Clara? He'd brought her out here to talk about Clara? Angela was glad that dusk prevented him from seeing the rise of color in her cheeks. Thank goodness he couldn't read her mind and the romantic notions she carried there. It all became clear now. It should have made things easier but it didn't.

"No, I didn't. She only arrived this morning, Sam."

"Still, you've known her for a while. She would have gone through screening, right?"

"Of course."

"She's perfect, Angela. Mom was incredibly easy to convince."

Angela pulled her fingers from his grasp. She came back to earth with a crash. Of course. A man like Sam—a woman like her. She was building castles in the air that didn't exist. She had never had to worry. Her feelings were her own and not returned, and therefore easily managed. She schooled her features and struggled to move back into professional mode. "Perfect for?"

"You know Mom needs help with Dad. Clara needs a job. And Dad likes her. He said so when we took him back to his room. For once he didn't argue with us. It took me a long time to convince Mom that she needed to hire help, but after meeting Clara… Her qualifications are perfect for what we need. What do you think?"

It was a wonderful opportunity and she was happy for Clara, of course. It was exactly what the program was designed for, and Molly would be a wonderful boss. Angela had no reservations about that whatsoever, except the sinking sensation that Clara would be spending her days in the glorious house surrounded by the warmth of the Diamonds. She didn't begrudge it one bit—Clara deserved it after what she'd been through. But Angela couldn't help feeling the tiniest bit envious.

"I think it's a terrific gesture and very generous of you," she replied, staring out over the dark fields. "I'll talk to Clara about it tomorrow."

"Thanks. It's been a productive day, hasn't it? First the open house, now this. Your project is off to a roaring start."

It was true, so why on earth was she feeling so empty? She should be happy, energized, raring to go. And instead she was weary. The fulfillment she expected wasn't as bright and shiny as she'd hoped.

"Thanks to you and your family."

He took her hand again and his dark eyes were earnest in the shadows. She froze the image on her mind so she could recall it later. This was feeling very much like a cutting of the strings, and it was necessary. But now and again she'd like to remember how he looked at this moment.

"It's all down to you. Being able to help was an honor," he finished quietly.

"Sam…" Tears pricked her eyelids and she looked down at her feet.

"I want to stay on the board."

Her gaze snapped to his. He what? But today was supposed to be the end. Especially if his parents hired Clara, there was no reason why Molly couldn't resume her position. Why on earth would he want to stay? And how difficult was it going to be seeing him on a regular basis? She didn't have any experience with this type of longing. Surely it would fade over time, wouldn't it?

"What about Diamondback, and your own concerns?"

"I've managed so far. A lot of the worry has been about Mom. If she has help now, that will take a load off my mind."

"But what about the biogas facility? I know how much that means to you."

"I doubt it will happen now. Mom has Power of Attorney, but there's nothing wrong with Dad's mind. And even if she could, she wouldn't go against his wishes. I don't know how to convince him. I've tried everything. I don't want to give up, but I've stopped having a timeline about it. It's too frustrating."

"I'm sorry."

"You control the things you can and let go of the rest, right? You made me see that it's not worth losing my dad over. We need to look after him first and then perhaps revisit the idea. So, you see, I will have some spare time to give the foundation. I thought you'd be glad."

Glad? The idea that she'd see him regularly was sweet torture. She was smart enough to know he wasn't doing it for her. They had no future. They were committed to different things in different places. They needed things that they couldn't provide for each other.

"Of course. My first priority is the foundation, and the connection to your family has been so beneficial." She wondered if she sounded as cold as the words made her seem.

"Beneficial." The word was flat. "That's all you have to say?"

She fidgeted with her fingers, unsure of what he wanted her to say. "Today couldn't have happened without you. I just hope you're doing it for the right reasons."

And not because you kissed me, she was tempted to add, but didn't. The less they referenced that kiss, the better. Men like Sam didn't set as much store in a simple kiss as she did. He'd probably already forgotten it.

He reached out and took her fingers loosely in his. "I'm doing it because helping you this last month has changed me. I enjoyed it. I realized today that I am proud of what we've done. What you're doing is so amazing, Angela. I just want to be a part of it a little longer."

His fingers were warm and strong. "You thought I was a hoity-toity do-gooder," she whispered.

"I was wrong."

"Sam, I…"

"We make a good team, Angela. Admit it."

She took a step backward, needing to put a few inches between herself and his seductive voice. She bit down on her lip. Sam Diamond could convince her of nearly anything, she realized, and that scared her. It made her feel weak and malleable. But she could not admit to him just how much he meant to her. The idea of having him on the board, involved with the house, made her feel weak. There was no way to explain it to him, either, not without revealing her true insecurities and she'd rather die than do that. "But your mom. The board position was hers."

"The deal was that a family member must sit on the board. It doesn't have to be Mom."

The owl hooted again, the sound lonely and mysterious.

"What are you so afraid of?" he asked quietly, squeezing her fingers.

She inhaled, decided on the truth. "You."

The air around them seemed to pause until Angela realized she was holding her breath, and she let it out slowly. Sam hadn't released her hand. She was so very aware of his body only inches from hers and the urge to step closer fought with her long-time instinct to flee. She'd let him get too close already.

"Me? Don't you know by now I'd never hurt you?"

She didn't mean that way, though perhaps it was easier. After all, that sort of fear was a tangible thing. Admitting she was afraid of her own feelings would be like touching a match to paper.

"You d-don't understand," she stammered, pulling her fingers away again and taking a step backward.

"Then make me understand. Make me understand what happened that night with the curtain rod. What happened yesterday when I kissed you? What's happening right now?"

He was asking questions that she didn't know how to answer, questions she'd spent years avoiding by not getting close to anyone. She shook her head. "I thought we were talking about board positions."

"Only if you're trying to avoid what's really happening here," he said, taking a step toward her and closing the distance once again.

"You said you wanted to be a part of Butterfly House."

"And I do. But not just that. Don't you understand? It's you, Angela."

"No." The word came out stronger than she expected. "You can't use the position to get closer to me. I don't come with the package."

"What has got you so terrified?" He reached out and laid his palm against her cheek. She wanted to trust him. She wanted to so much it hurt in places she hadn't let herself feel for years.

"I care about you," he murmured, taking one more step so that their bodies hovered a mere breath apart. "I didn't want to. You know that. But I do. I don't know what to do about it, but I know I don't want to stop. When I'm with you everything makes sense."

He was going to kiss her. She knew it even before he began to dip his head. Her lips started to tingle in anticipation and they parted as her eye-lids drifted closed.

She would let him kiss her one last time. And then he'd walk away. She'd make sure of it.

CHAPTER NINE

THE heat of his body warmed the air between them as he drew her closer, while the cool summer breeze ruffled the hem of her skirt. Hot and cold, light and dark. They were as different as two people could be, and maybe that was part of the attraction. Sam was all the things that Angela had never been—strong, confident, sure of his place in the world. It was no wonder she was drawn to him like a moth to a flame. As his lips grazed hers, she caught her breath and decided to enjoy the moment. She could always pull away before she got singed by the fire.

He cupped her face in his hands. So softly she could hardly bear it, he kissed the corner of her mouth, her cheek, her temple. His long fingers slid down over her jawbone and he paused. Angela put her hand on his shoulder and felt the tension vibrating there. He was holding back. The idea of all that leashed energy was vastly exciting and a very

feminine part of her was wooed by the consider-
ation that was costing him so much.

She wound her arms around his neck and placed
her mouth on his.

Taking the initiative changed the dynamic of
the contact instantly. After a heartbeat of surprise,
Sam opened his lips and kissed her fully, wrapping
his arms around her middle and lifting her off the
ground until only the tips of her toes touched the
grass. There was no hope of surviving unsinged
now. Her whole body felt as though it was on fire,
with the soft sounds of their kisses in the dark fan-
ning the flames.

She let her fingers run through his short hair,
adoring the silky warmth of it and feeling a jolt of
desire as he made a sound of arousal deep in his
throat. He held her against the planes of his workingman's body, long and lean and muscular, until
she felt they must be imprinted on her own. It was
the most glorious thing she had ever experienced.
Even as she knew they had to stop, she didn't want
to. Just a few seconds more before she had to give
it all up. She was hungry and hadn't yet had her
fill.

Slowly he lowered her to the ground so she was
standing on both feet again. He linked his hands at
the hollow of her back, holding her in the circle of
his arms while he continued to sip from her lips.

Finally she broke away, knowing she couldn't

let it go on any longer and still retain her dignity. She'd practically thrown herself into his arms, conveniently forgetting all the reasons why it was a mistake. Heat rushed into her face and she pressed her hands to her cheeks. Her heart drummed insistently against her ribs. His wary eyes watched her but the rest of his body remained completely still as she took a step backward.

He was too much, too powerful, too attractive. He made her want things, different things than she'd wanted for as long as she could remember. She'd known from the beginning he was going to be trouble. She just hadn't thought he'd be *this* kind of trouble.

"Sam," she chastised quietly. "We can't."

"Why?" He crossed his arms over his chest. The pose highlighted his muscled arms and she licked her lips. She wouldn't respond to his physicality. She had to keep her head. One of them had to.

"This is too complicated. There are so many reasons why we shouldn't."

"Is that right?" His voice was soft and seductive. "You know, I've been trying to figure out what it is about you that sets me off."

He put his hands in his back pockets, highlighting the breadth of his chest and shoulders. That restless energy that couldn't be tamed was sparking through the air again, making it come alive.

Making *her* come alive, and she wasn't prepared for it.

"I don't mean to set you off," she replied in a small voice.

"But you do," he said softly. "You challenge me. You're *work.* You have firm opinions, and I respect you for them."

He took a step forward, relaxing his arms, treating her to a small, sideways smile. He reached out and ran a finger over her arm, raising the delicate hairs and goosebumps beneath his touch. "Something's happening between us, Angela. It started that night with the curtains. Don't deny it."

She stepped back. "Don't, please," she said, embarrassingly aroused and horribly tempted to give in. She imagined what would come next, out here in the soft darkness. She hadn't been intimate with a man in... She blinked as she stared into Sam's determined face. In a very long time. It had nearly cost her everything—and she'd nearly lost herself in the process. She couldn't do that again.

"It's not just wanting you, you know that, right?" His eyes gleamed at her. "It's the way you see the world. It's how you make me stop and think. Like with the kids today. I looked at them and saw trouble but you made me see something else—potential. With Clara, too." He smiled gently. "I never considered myself narrow-minded, but you make me look beyond the surface. That's why I'm fall..."

"Stop," she commanded, cutting him off before he could say any more. Her pulse hammered at her throat. She didn't know how to do this. She didn't know how to care about someone this much or—worse—accept that they might care about her. She was as emotionally stunted as any of her clients only she was able to give it a proper name and she'd had years of practice at covering it. He couldn't fall for her, and she couldn't fall for him either.

"You're afraid."

Sam knew nothing about what really drove her, and it took her breath away to realize how close she was to telling him the whole truth. To trusting him. Her heart told her she could but her head kept her mouth shut. She'd learned long ago that her heart had flawed judgment.

"I'm not afraid," she replied, forcing herself to stand tall as she lied. "What I am is leaving."

She turned to walk away and he reached out, his strong fingers circling her wrist. "Don't go. Talk to me."

This time there was no fear, only temptation to fall back into his embrace. A part of her thrilled to hear the words. But a stronger, more rational part had a bigger voice. She wrenched her wrist out of his grasp, panic rising at the dull pain that shot through her arm as she twisted it away. Panic that he would somehow see through her, leaving her vulnerable and exposed. He wanted more from her than she could ever give.

"I have to. I got carried away in the moonlight for a minute but it's over." She began to back away, feeling the cool grass against her toes as she stepped off the path. "Please, just let me go. Don't come after me and don't call, Sam."

"But, Angela…"

"Just don't." Her voice choked. "I can't, don't you see?"

"No, goddammit, I don't!" He ran his hand over his hair and heaved out a breath. "Tell me what you're so afraid of. Let me help you."

"I can't." She gave him one last desperate glance before turning and fleeing. Not even the twinges in her toe slowed her down until she reached the steps of the back deck.

The glow from the kitchen lights filtered weakly over the grass and there was a muffled bark that sounded from inside—the Diamonds' dog was in for the night now that dark had fallen fully. Angela saw Molly's figure pass in front of the French doors and she hesitated, knowing she had to go in and collect Clara and her purse, needing to catch her breath first.

The motion light over the door came on as she climbed the stairs. She hurried to school her features into what she hoped was a pleasant smile before turning the handle on the door and entering the warm kitchen that still smelled of fresh bread and chocolate cake.

No one would ever know just how close she'd come to losing her head tonight. And even though she knew leaving was the right thing, she'd hold the sweet memory of this evening—all of it—inside during the months ahead. She was so used to being on the outside, staring longingly through the window at the perfect life she'd never have.

For one magical night, Sam had shown her what it could be like on the inside.

To Angela's surprise, Sam heeded her plea to leave her alone as July turned to August and Butterfly House became a buzz of activity. He was nowhere to be seen as three more tenants arrived and Angela's days were full with the day-to-day running of the project. Clara began working days at the Diamonds', looking after Virgil. She came home at night with stories about the family, tidbits that made Angela feel connected to Sam in some small way.

They also made her miss him horribly. She kept telling herself it was for the best, but there was no denying that she got an empty feeling every time a car turned into the yard and it wasn't him.

Then there were the handymen.

The first day the crew arrived Angela was in her office, conducting a session with her latest resident,

Jane. She excused herself to see what was going on and found three men unloading scaffolding and paint.

"What do you think you're doing?"

"Mornin', ma'am. Just about to start working on your trim. We'll have it spruced up in no time."

She didn't want to sound rude but there was clearly some mistake. "But I didn't hire you."

"No, ma'am. Mr. Diamond did. We're to paint the gingerbread trim and stain the porch and railings." He put down the gallons of paint in his hand and straightened, wiping his hands on his coveralls. "Might want to use the back door until it's done."

She hesitated. Sam should have asked her first before going ahead with anything. The trouble was the trim did need a coat of paint and the porch, while sturdier since his repairs, made the house look shabby. A tiny voice inside her head asked her what she'd expected. Why would Sam ask her approval if she'd told him flat out to leave her alone?

Sending the men away would cause more trouble than it was worth. "All right then, go ahead. I'll be inside if you need anything."

"Yes, ma'am," he replied, and motioned to the others to begin setting up the scaffolding.

Angela had firmly believed that the whole out-of-sight, out-of-mind thing would work, but she felt Sam's presence constantly. After the workmen finished, one of the local teens came by to mow the grass and asked if he could put the new pushmower Mr. Diamond had provided in the shed when he was finished. The house and yard looked better than ever but, inside, her emotions were churning. Mr. Diamond this and Mr. Diamond that. Exorcising him from her thoughts proved harder than she'd expected. He'd helped with the fixing-up, and now it seemed that his handiwork was all around her, whether she asked for it or not.

The final straw was the feature in the local monthly paper. It had carried a wonderful spot on the project, but it was the picture they'd used of her with Sam that made her heart catch. It hadn't been one of the posed shots. Instead the black-and-white photo that stared up at her from the newsprint was one where Sam was looking back at her and she was grinning down at him—when they'd been teasing each other. He'd been a royal pain in the behind and a bright light in her life all at once, and now everything was gray and dull in his absence.

She folded the paper and put it in a desk drawer. The feature was good, though she wished it had focused more about the foundation and less about her. Sam had done a bang-up job singing her praises and her name was everywhere. She told herself she shouldn't worry. No one in Edmonton even cared where she was now. And the two people who might—well, Angela had stopped deluding herself long ago. The chances of Jack Beck actually reading a small-town rag were slim to none. The anxiety was natural, she supposed, but not necessarily rational.

But the picture of her with Sam was branded on her mind. She lay awake one hot summer night, her window open as she listened to the sounds of the peepers in the nearby slough and the rustle of the leaves. Coyotes howled, the sound so plaintive and lonely that she felt like howling along with them. She flipped over, punching her pillow, but her eyes remained stubbornly open. She couldn't erase the image of Sam in the moonlight, his lips still slightly swollen from her kisses. She had to do something, so she got out of bed and went downstairs in her pajamas. When she couldn't sleep, she baked. And when she was this twitchy, only one recipe would do.

She was careful to be quiet as she whisked together the cream, sugar and cocoa over the burner for the chocolate silk filling. A baked crust cooled on the counter as she stirred, wishing she could stir away her thoughts as easily as the whisk smoothed away the lumps in the mixture.

She poured the thickened filling into the crust and scraped the sides of the pan with her spatula. She gave the plastic surface an indulgent lick—the secret was in the melted dark chocolate—and then put both pot and spatula in the sink before turning back to the fridge and sliding the pie in to set. She stretched and gave a huge yawn. Baking always did the trick. Tomorrow morning would be time enough to whip up the cream for the top and they could all have a treat.

She was just wiping the pan dry when there was a horrible pounding on the door.

For one terrified second she couldn't move, flooded by a hundred memories crowding her consciousness all at once. This was the reality she knew—that no amount of therapy or time ever completely erased the fear, especially the reflexive reaction in that moment before rational thought took over. The pounding persisted and she forced her feet to move, grabbing the handset to the phone on the way by. Just in case.

Steps echoed behind her as Clara, Jane, Alyssa and Sue rattled down the stairs. When Angela reached the door, she turned and looked at the women standing behind her, their eyes wide, cheeks pale. Whatever Angela was feeling, it had to be a hundred times worse for them. It was fresher for them and they were looking to her to set an example. She squared her shoulders and peeped through the Judas hole.

What she saw turned her knees to jelly.

She flipped the locks and opened the door, her stomach turning and heart pounding as she looked down at the woman on her knees on the front step.

"Mom?"

Beverly Beck lifted her head and Angela's soul wept at the sight of her. One eye was so swollen it was closed, while the opposite cheek sported an angry red bruise. Her bottom lip was cracked and when Angela knelt and touched her arm, she started to cry.

Angela felt an anger so profound she thought she might explode out of her own skin with it. This woman—this kind, caring woman who had done nothing but give blind devotion to her husband— had been repaid with *this*.

"Come inside," she whispered, going out carefully. "Let me help you."

Gently she helped her mother get to her feet and led her inside. She shut the door and locked it and nodded at the group of women still standing in the kitchen. "It's all right," she said, trying to sound reassuring while the conflicting mass of emotions tied knots in her belly. "We'll be in my office," she said, leading Beverly into the small room off the entry.

Beverly was still crying quietly and Angela led her to a small couch. They sat side by side and she simply waited for her mother to speak. When Beverly was ready, she patted Angela's hand and sighed.

"Help me, Angie," she said.

Angela had waited her whole life to hear that

simple request, and her heart seemed to burst hearing the words.

No matter the hurt or blame that she had held inside over the years, this was her mother. The woman who had cut flower shapes out of sandwiches with cookie cutters when she was a child, the one who had taken her on weekly trips to the library until Angela was old enough to go on her own. She was the one who, no matter what, tucked Angela into bed at night and promised that tomorrow would be better even if she never kept those promises. Somewhere inside this broken body that beautiful woman still existed, and Angela opened her arms. "Of course I'll help you," she murmured, kissing her mother's graying hair. "It's all I've ever wanted."

There was a discreet knock on the door and Clara poked her head inside. "I made a pot of tea," she said quietly. "I thought you might like some."

"That'd be lovely—thank you." Angela sat back, wiping her fingers under her eyes and then took Beverly's hands in her own. She noticed that her mother's nails were short and chipped, her hands chapped. How many horrors had she suffered in the years since Angela left? Not for the first time, she felt unbearable guilt for leaving her mother to face things on her own.

Clara returned with a tray containing a teapot,

mugs, milk and a plate of toast with a jar of jam.
"In case someone would like a bite," she offered.

"Thank you, Clara." She offered a small smile,
wanting to inject as much normalcy into the evening as she could. "Is everyone okay?" Clara was
turning out to be a truly nurturing soul. The Diamonds were lucky to have her.

"A little shaken, but okay. They're going back to
bed now."

"I'll see you in the morning, then."

Clara shut the door with a quiet click.

The new silence was deafening.

Angela poured two cups of tea and added milk
to each. "Here," she offered, holding out the cup.
"Drink this. You'll feel better and you can tell me
what happened."

Beverly offered no resistance as she wrapped her
hands around the warm mug and Angela wondered
if she'd simply been used to obeying for so long
that she didn't know how to do anything else. For
the first time since becoming a social worker, Angela felt as though she was in over her head, flying
by the seat of her pants.

The tea was hot and reviving, and she caught
her mother's gaze focused on the toast. Angela
wondered when she'd eaten last. She knew very
well that there wasn't always money for groceries.
"Jam?"

She spread a triangle with saskatoonberry jam and handed it over.

When the piece was gone, Angela sat up straighter. "You're not here for tea and toast. Can you tell me what happened?"

Beverly nodded. "I left your father."

"After he did this to you." The words came out tightly, like the string of a bow held taut, ready for release.

Another nod.

"Have you left him for good?"

Angela held her breath. The answer had to be yes. Beverly couldn't come this far and then go back, could she? But Angela knew she could. How many times had they talked about packing a bag and disappearing? It was always too good to be true. She had to attempt to keep her own feelings out of the mix right now. She had to if she were truly going to help.

Fear widened Beverly's eyes but she nodded once more. "I packed a bag tonight when he was at the bar. I took the car and came here."

Oh, Lord. Beverly hadn't had a driver's license for over fifteen years. If she'd been stopped she would have ended up right back home again. And Angela wouldn't put it past her father to report the vehicle stolen. Wouldn't it be ironic if the police were the ones to deliver her back to her doorstep?

Angela looked at Beverly's downturned head and said slowly, "Does he know *where* you've gone?"

Agonized eyes met hers. "I don't know."

Something in the tone, and the way her mother's eyes dropped once more to her lap, made a line of dread sneak down Angela's spine. There was something more. "What set him off this time? What changed?"

Beverly's gaze skittered away again. "It doesn't matter."

"Mom."

Beverly's fingers picked at the frayed hem of her blouse. "I cut out that picture of you in the paper. I couldn't believe it was you, honey. You're so grown-up and pretty. I read all about this place and I was real proud, you know?"

Everything came crashing down. This was her fault, wasn't it? She hadn't realized the story had been picked up by the city paper. The words were like little knives cutting through Angela's skin, sharp and stinging. Why couldn't this have happened years ago when she'd begged and pleaded? Maybe they could have done this together. Maybe…

But Angela knew that the world didn't run on maybes. She forced the useless wish aside. "And?"

"Your dad, he found the picture and got right ugly."

"And he took it out on you."

There was no answer to give. They both knew

she was right. Ever since the day Angela had left, there'd been no one but Beverly for him to use as a punching bag.

And ever since that day Angela had worked so hard, trying to atone for it.

"He told me to remember my place, and..." Her throat worked but no words came out for a moment. "When he was done with me he took off to the usual watering hole. I wasn't going to come, but he said he should have made you pay years ago. I was so scared, Angela. Afraid of what he might do. Afraid that he'd...he'd use me to get to you again."

Another thick silence fell. Neither of them needed to say the words. They both knew he'd already used Beverly to get to Angela.

"So he knows where I am. What I do?"

"It made him some mad."

A cold finger of fear shivered down Angela's spine, followed by anger. She couldn't let him have this power over her anymore. Not just her, either. There were four other women—five counting Beverly—looking to her for strength and leadership. She couldn't let them down. She didn't know what to do—everything seemed to be crumbling inside. Beverly put her hand over her face and started weeping again, the sound full of despair and hopelessness.

Angela's insides were quaking and she knew she couldn't do this alone.

Her first call should be to the police, but she couldn't make herself dial the number. The very thought of it was exhausting and left her emotionally drained. There was only one thing—one person—she wanted. It probably wasn't wise, and it definitely didn't make sense after their last conversation, but right now she would give anything to see Sam's strong face.

She got up from the couch, went to the desk drawer and pulled out a scrap of paper that she'd kept since the day she'd dropped the box spring on her toe. *If you need anything,* he'd said, *call me.*

With a tangle of nerves in her stomach, she dialed Sam's cell number.

CHAPTER TEN

THE shrill ringtone of his cell dragged him out of a dead sleep and set his heart pounding. He reached for the phone beside the bed and fumbled with the buttons. A sane person never called at this hour unless something was wrong.

"Yuh, hello," he said into the phone, rubbing his hand over his face.

"It's Angela."

His eyes snapped open. There was something wrong. It was in the tight, odd sound to her voice. Like she was trying to sound normal but there was an edge to it that hinted of hysteria. He sat up in bed, fully alert, and reached over to turn on the bedside lamp. "What's going on?"

"Can you come over?"

There was a quiver in the last word as her voice caught. No preamble, no explanation, no wasted words, just a plea that put a cold shiver into his heart. The Angela he knew would have been rational and explained. She never would have been so raw and vulnerable. Or afraid. He was sure she was afraid for some reason. "Are you all right?"

"I just…I need you."

Goddamn. The last time they'd spoken she'd told him to leave her alone and he'd granted that request. For her to turn to him now had to mean something was desperately wrong. "Give me ten minutes," he replied, hanging up at the same time as he launched himself out of bed and reached for his jeans.

He drove far too fast in the dark, trying to think of plausible scenarios for why she'd call him in the middle of the night. Running the sort of place she did, his first reaction was that an ex-husband or boyfriend had caused trouble. He swallowed, putting his foot on the gas. Was someone hurt? Angela? Or Clara? She'd been such a bright spot around the house. Clara's help had made such a difference with Virgil. The very thought of her being in trouble was horrible. But when he thought of Angela, it was different. There was fear for her, but something more. A desire to protect her. Even though weeks had passed since they'd kissed in the garden, it was far from over. Not for Sam. It was time he admitted the truth to himself. He'd fallen in love with her, he'd blown it and he had no idea what to do next.

He was there in seven minutes flat. He knocked on the door and then tried the knob. It was locked, so he knocked a little louder. A strange car sat in the driveway and he set his jaw. If someone didn't answer soon, he'd break in the door if he had to.

Clara answered, wrapped up in a housecoat and slippers. Her face was pale but she offered Sam a weak smile. "She called you. I'm glad. Come in, Sam."

He followed her inside, glad she was clearly unhurt. "What's going on?"

Angela's office door opened and she stepped into the hall. For a moment all he could see were the tearstains on her cheeks. In the next heartbeat she was in his arms.

He took a step backward as the force of her embrace took him by surprise. He closed his eyes and put his arms around her. Lordy, she felt like she'd lost weight, she was so small and fragile. Her shoulders rose and fell and he heard her sniffle against his shirt. She was not a woman who surrendered easily; now she was crying in his arms. He held her tighter, wanting to protect her from whatever was pulling her apart at the seams.

There was no sense denying it now, no sense fighting what he'd been trying to ignore for weeks. He'd do anything for her. And right now he sensed that what she needed was a gentle touch. "Shhh," he offered, rubbing her back through her thin T-shirt. "What's wrong, Ang? You have to tell me what's wrong."

She lifted her head. "I…" She drew in a shuddering breath. "I shouldn't be so glad to see you, but I am."

A woman stepped out of the office, peering timidly around the corner. Sam saw the cracked lip and bruises and felt as though he'd been punched in the gut for the second time in as many minutes. She looked startled as she met his gaze and went back inside, but she turned a little, showing her profile. A profile that was remarkably similar to the woman in his arms, if she were a few decades older.

He ran his hand over her hair, suddenly understanding why she was so upset. "Is that your mom?"

Angela turned her head quickly but the woman had already gone back inside, shutting the door with a quiet click.

"Yes," she answered. "Yes, that's my mother. She showed up tonight after my father lit into her. For the last time, if I have anything to say about it."

Shock rippled through him as she admitted the truth. He knew how passionate she was about Butterfly House, how committed she was to ending abuse and helping these women start over. But her own mother… She had to be devastated. He was gutted just looking at the bruises. How must she feel as her daughter? How would he feel if it were Molly? Questions zinged through his mind, piling one on top of the other. Had she known? Had it been going on all through Angela's childhood? Had she been a victim of her father's abuse, too? His stomach turned. How much had she suffered? And then there was the relationship she mentioned. How did that fit into everything? How much had she truly hidden from him?

But the answers would have to wait. They had to deal with the right now first.

Angela wouldn't push him away this time. No matter what it took. No matter how much she might fight him on it. The days of her standing alone against the world were done.

"Tell me what you need," he said, tipping up her chin with a finger and meeting her gaze. "Tell me what I can do to help and I'll do it."

Angela lost herself in his dark gaze for just a moment. Never before had she let herself need someone this much. Not just need—but she'd willingly placed herself in the hands of another and it was terrifying and a relief all at once.

It was scary to surrender when she'd spent her whole life avoiding that very thing. But also terrifying in how *right* it felt. It filled her with a sense of certainty that she'd never experienced before. She knew that Sam would be there. She'd known it the day he'd given her his cell number and told her to call if she needed anything. It had gone beyond items on a grocery list. It had even gone beyond a kiss in the moonlight.

She reached up and circled his wrist with her fingers, drawing his hand away from her face. Right now she was just happy to have him there. "I need your advice."

She wanted someone objective to look at the situation, someone whose life hadn't been colored by abusive situations. It stung her pride to know that she'd lost her objectivity. But some things were more important than pride. Like safety for all of them.

He looked startled, uncomfortable as he drew back a little and furrowed his brow. "Are you sure I'm the right person to ask? I have no experience with this."

She didn't share his doubts. "I can manage my mom. I think. But it's my father." She filled him in on the events of the evening. "And so you see, she took the car. She has no license, no insurance. He could report the car stolen. He'll be angry, Sam, and I'm not sure what to do next." She fought against the finger of fear that trickled down her spine and the backs of her legs. "He'll be really angry. And…" She swallowed. "He knows where I am. Because of the article and my picture."

"This is my fault," he murmured, his face flattening with shock. "I pushed you into being in that photo. You didn't even want to do it. Oh, Angela."

"It's not your fault, I promise."

"But…"

Things became very clear for Angela in that moment. Sam was blaming himself just as she'd blamed herself for years. "Look at me," she said, her voice stronger than she thought possible. "It's easy to blame yourself. You play the 'if only' game. 'If only I had done something differently.' 'If only I hadn't said that.' But the truth is abusers like my dad don't really need reasons. It is not your fault, Sam. It's his, and his alone. I promise."

There was freedom with the words, but she also felt her energy being sapped from the high emotion of the events. "But that doesn't change what we're dealing with." She pressed her fingers to the bridge of her nose, feeling the beginnings of a headache. "It won't take him long to figure out where she went."

"Did you call the police?"

"I've only called you. He won't realize she's gone until he gets home from the bar, maybe not until he wakes up with a hangover."

She couldn't help the bitterness that flavored the words. She knew the routine well. Jack would come home smelling like tequila and cigarettes and pass out. It was the next morning that was the worst. When the shakes set in along with the anger.

"But he needs to be arrested."

Nausea turned in Angela's stomach. "I…"

Her voice abandoned her and she looked at her feet.

Sam didn't speak for several long seconds. Finally he said the words down low. "Are you still afraid of him?"

"I left, didn't I?"

"Oh, honey. It's not the same thing, and we both know it. Look at me, please."

She lifted her head and met his gaze, hot shame filling her as she bit down on her lip.

"It's one thing to accept you're not to blame, but quite another to look down the barrel of the gun, isn't it?"

She didn't want to agree, so she kept silent. There were too many years and too many scars. She wanted to say she didn't care, that she wasn't afraid. But she was.

"If this were any other woman, would you hesitate to call the police?"

They both knew the answer. She'd made the phone call many, many times over the years.

"I can't," she whispered. "Oh, Sam, I'm such a hypocrite. I run this place and pretend I'm all whole and everything. But when it comes down to it, I'm still…" Tears clogged her throat. "A victim."

"Those women have you as their champion. But you had no one." He cupped her chin in his fingers.

"Until now. You have me. And you are not going to do this alone."

She wouldn't cry. Not anymore. She needed to be strong and deal with what needed to be dealt with. And right now her first priority was her mother.

"I've got to be with her," she murmured. "She's so fragile right now. So scared."

"You look after your mom and I'll look after the rest," Sam said, drawing himself up to his full height. He was an imposing sight, her protector. She had never wanted to admit she needed a guardian, but she was glad to have him tonight. There wasn't a spare ounce that wasn't solid muscle and the glint in his eye and angle of his jaw spoke of determination. She'd pegged him as being stubborn before, blindly so. But now she knew he was not. He simply fought for those things he believed in. And tonight she was fortunate he believed in her and Butterfly House.

"I need to get her settled. This isn't the place for her. In the morning I'll need to get her to a different kind of shelter. It's a different sort of help here. And she's going to need me beside her."

"You do that and I'll make some phone calls. Don't worry, Ang. I won't let him hurt either of you. I promise."

She swallowed past the lump in her throat. Sam always made good on his promises. She knew that by now.

"You'll wait for me, then?"

He nodded. "Of course I will."

"There's tea in the kitchen."

His lopsided smile nearly popped a dimple. "I think I could use a whiskey, but I know the rules. Tea will do."

She stepped away from him and took three shaky steps back to her office before turning back.

"Thank you for coming," she murmured, her hand resting on the door frame. "I don't know how I would have gotten through this without you."

Then she turned away before she could hear his response. Because the look in his eyes was so tender and caring she suddenly felt at risk of exposing everything.

And that was something she just couldn't do.

When Beverly was settled in the last unoccupied bedroom, Angela shut the door gently and finally let her shoulders slump. If they could get through this first night it would be better. For a few panicked minutes her mother had insisted on going home, saying that it would be better than Jack's fury when he found out what she'd done. That he'd forgive her—as if she somehow needed forgiveness. Jack—Angela had long ago stopped thinking of him as Dad—was the one who should be on his knees. It had taken all of Angela's energy to

stay calm and logical when she still felt her own
fear and anger.

But she bit her tongue and was soothing and rational and all the other important things she needed
to be, knowing that Sam waited. She might be weak
but she would do this. They hadn't come this far to
mess it up now.

She had tended to Beverly's wounds and helped
her to bed, assuring her mother it would all be
fine, while inside she held no such guarantee. This
wasn't the end. It was only the beginning. And
she still listened with one ear, wondering if Jack
would come along and pound on her door and start
making demands. That couldn't happen. Not just
for Beverly but for the other women. This was
supposed to be their safe place. She leaned back
against the bedroom door and closed her eyes. That
open house was supposed to be such a positive
thing. Something to build awareness and support.
And now because of her, it could all come tumbling down.

When she entered the kitchen, she was shocked
to see Sam casually washing up the dishes from
the tea and toast. A dish towel was slung over his
shoulder as he washed out the teapot and rinsed it
beneath the hot spray. There was something both
masculine and nurturing about it and she knew
she was in horrible danger of falling in love with
him despite all her precautions. The phone call

and embrace had been simple reactions to an extremely stressful situation, but even Angela, in her emotional state, realized that she never would have done either if something deeper weren't at work.

Love. A lump formed in her throat. It was impossible.

"I can do those in the morning," she said, wrapping her arms around her middle. She was still in the pink boxers and T-shirt she'd worn to answer the door and while perfectly modest, felt quite exposed beneath his dark gaze.

He slid the dish towel off his shoulder, gave the pot a wipe and put it down on the counter. "It was no trouble. I needed to do something while I waited."

"I kept you a long time."

His gaze was far too understanding for her to be comfortable. "You had a good reason. Do you want tea? I can make a new pot."

She shook her head. At the moment, his earlier suggestion of whiskey sounded just about right, but she had a policy about alcohol on the premises. "No, I'm fine. I had some earlier."

"Is your mom asleep?"

Angela shrugged. "I don't know. I figure she'll either lie awake a long time, or she'll be so exhausted she'll conk out completely." She moved farther into the room, forcing deep breaths to keep from feeling overwhelmed. "She's here, and that's the main thing."

"Well, no one's going to bother you tonight."

There was an edge to his voice, a defiance that sent a little fizz through her veins. "You don't have to stay, Sam. You've done so much already." She felt obligated to say it even as the thought of him leaving made an empty hole form inside her.

"You can't get rid of me that easily," he replied. He hung the dish towel over the oven-door handle. "I called a friend of mine. The car's been towed and it'll be delivered back to Edmonton like it had never gone missing. Then I called Mike Kowal-chuk. He was here at the open house, remember? The constable. He's aware of the situation and he's contacted the police in the city. Someone's going to be watching the street until your dad is picked up. No one will get within a hundred yards without Mike knowing."

Relief swamped her. "I had no idea…"

"We take care of our own around here."

And he included her as one of them. The fact that he'd gotten people out of bed and into action with a few simple phone calls wasn't lost on her. When Sam wanted something done, he didn't stop until he made it happen. It was intimidating—and embarrassing that he'd had to do what she normally would have done in this situation. She was thankful for the support even as she felt like he was taking over.

She didn't like being the one not in control.

"I don't know what to say."

"Don't say anything." He stepped forward and cupped her face in his palm. "Keeping you safe comes first," he said simply.

She stared at his lips, wondering if he was going to kiss her, wondering if she even truly wanted him to.

Instead he pressed his lips to her forehead. They were firm and warm and reassuring. "You must have been so scared," he murmured.

"Not the first time. Or the worst," she said quietly.

He uttered a curse and ran a hand over his jaw. "I didn't know."

She took pity on him then, not liking the awkward silence that had fallen over the kitchen. "How could you? I've never told anyone. Don't worry about it." She sighed, feeling so much older than her years. "My mother has been in the same situation for as long as I can remember."

"I'm worried about you. You're pale and exhausted. You should rest."

"I'm fine. Everything's fine now." She pushed away and wished she had a housecoat, a hoodie, anything to make her feel less naked.

"If you're fine, why do you look like you're about to collapse?"

He had her there. She wasn't fine. She was nowhere near fine. And she wouldn't be for a long time. Most days her energy went into current projects and she could forget—or ignore—those very real incidents that had shaped her past. But tonight she'd come face-to-face with her demons again. And relived every moment when she'd opened the front door and wondered what she'd find inside.

She blinked rapidly as his shape blurred. All the adrenaline abandoned her and exactly what had happened truly, finally, sank in. The life she had left behind had caught up with her. But her mother was out and had made that important first step. It shouldn't hurt this much to get what she'd always wanted.

"It's okay," she heard him say gently. "Aw, baby, come here."

He opened his arms.

She went to him because now that it was over she was fragile. He hugged her close and she drank in his smell—a bit woodsy, a bit like citrus and the blankety-soft scent of sleep because she'd dragged him out of bed.

"Come sit down before you fall down." His breath was warm on her ear and made her body shiver in an instinctive reaction. She had no energy left to fight him with, and, her hand tucked inside his, they went into the living room and sat side by side on the sofa.

"It's so hard," she confessed, and it felt so good to finally confide in someone. "It's not the same when it's your own mother, you know?" She closed her eyes and leaned against his shoulder. "At one point I thought she was going to get up and walk back out the door. I wanted to beg her not to go. I wanted to get down on my knees and plead with her not to let it happen again. But I learned a long time ago that begging doesn't work. So I sucked it up and put on my best social-worker hat. I was very professional on the outside," she continued, chancing a look up at him.

She realized for the first time that his shirt was buttoned incorrectly. She stared at the uneven buttons and her heart melted just a little. She'd frightened him that much, then, that he'd rushed into his clothes and raced over here without a second thought. She hadn't deserved that, not after the way she'd treated him. Not after the way she'd treat him before this was all over.

"And on the inside?"

She sighed. "On the inside I'm a mess. I'm supposed to be objective and smart and helpful. And you know what I am?"

He shook his head.

She looked down at her hands, not wanting to see disappointment in his eyes. "I'm a coward."

"You're the bravest woman I know," he replied, putting his arm around her shoulder, cuddling her in more as he leaned against the arm of the sofa. "Look at all you've accomplished here. Look at Clara, and the other women you're helping. Ang, at one time they arrived somewhere looking very much like your mother does tonight. Now look where they are."

Tonight was the first time he'd ever shortened her name. No one had ever called her Ang. Not ever. Not friends, not her mom, not even Steve when he'd been at his charming best and had sucked her into a controlling relationship. She liked the way it sounded when Sam said it, maybe too much.

"You don't understand."

"Then help me to."

Why did he have to be so wonderful? The last time they'd spoken she'd left him standing in the moonlight and told him to leave her alone. He'd followed her wishes to the letter, but he'd been taking care of her all along, she realized, helping her project when she refused any other sort of contact. He couldn't do that forever. At some point the emergency would be over and they'd have to get back to their regularly scheduled lives.

"Sam, what you saw tonight—that was my life, too. It was my daily existence from my first memories until I finished high school. I got a scholarship, packed my bags one night when my father was passed out, and never looked back."

"I wondered," he said quietly. "Tonight I was shocked, but not really surprised. There is something about you. A distance, a protective layer you never let down. You are always so determined to stand on your own two feet, never to back down. Like you have something to prove."

"Maybe I do." He was being rather insightful and she wasn't sure if she was glad at not having to explain or unsettled that she was so transparent.

"The only other time you let your guard down was the day before the open house."

Yes, the day she'd seen all her plans crumble before her eyes when that cursed box spring dropped on her foot. The day he'd turned her into a puddle of feminine goo and scared the hell out of her when he'd kissed her. "I felt safe, I suppose. Doesn't mean it was easy."

His hand rubbed along her arm, warm and reassuring, anchoring her to the present. After a few minutes, he spoke again. "He beat you, too, didn't he? That's why you were too afraid to make the call tonight."

"I don't want your pity," she warned. "There are a lot of ways to hurt a person, and not always with fists, though I had my share of those, too. I went to school and was around other people so Jack was careful not to leave any marks where they'd show.

Those bruises healed faster than the hateful words and names he called me."

Sam didn't answer. She knew it was a lot for him to take in, but maybe now he'd finally understand why things could never work between them. "A father is supposed to be a provider and protector, you know? He broke trust with my mother and with me."

"Yes, he did."

"And I left rather than confronting him about it. He was my father. I thought I should love him. That he should love me. But love isn't supposed to be like that. It was easier to leave than to deal with it. With him."

He seemed to consider for a moment. "But when you studied, when you became a social worker…"

"You mean that I should have figured this all out then, right? Fixed myself?" She gave a short laugh. "I thought I had, but that was before I really understood what…"

She stopped. She'd been about to say *what real love feels like.* It would have been a slip that was tantamount to a three-word declaration. And a big mistake. Maybe she was in love with him. And maybe it did change everything. But it didn't mean it would ever work and it was better to leave the words unsaid.

"Before I really understood," she repeated, hoping he wouldn't pursue the *what.*

"You must be happy that your mom has taken this step, then."

She sighed. "Of course. But that's not easy, either. I don't want to be angry with her but I am. She broke trust with me, too, Sam. I needed her to stand up. To leave. To put me first. She stayed, insisting that he loved her. I've been so angry, so helpless." Her lip wobbled. "So guilty."

"Guilty? What on earth do you have to feel guilty about?" He twisted a little so that he was looking down at her face. "That's crazy talk."

She shook her head. "I left her there, Sam. I left her alone to deal with Jack all by herself. How many beatings did she endure when he realized I was gone? How many since?" She put her head in her hands, feeling the awful truth wrapping its cords around her neck. "I was angry and I gave up on her."

"You listen to me," Sam said, taking her hands in his and removing them from her face. "Look at me."

She couldn't. She was this close to falling apart and looking at him would ensure it. Nothing he could say would convince her that this wasn't her fault. It was all true. She had given up on her mother. She'd written her off. She'd dedicated her life to helping abused women and she was an absolute farce.

"I said look at me."

She looked up.

He looked angry, she realized, but not in a frightening, threatening way. In a way that made her heart take a ridiculous leap. "You did not give up on her. What you did was survive."

"I sacrificed her for myself, Sam. It was utterly selfish."

"That's garbage and you know it. You just got finished telling me that it was not my fault. Well, it's not yours, either, and deep down you know it. You relied on her to protect you and when she didn't, you protected yourself. That's courageous and smart, and don't let anyone tell you differently. You were a *kid*. You dedicated your life to helping women like your mom. And I'm guessing there are a lot of people out there thankful for whatever selfishness, as you call it, that you demonstrated. You've saved lives, Angela Beck. So do not sell yourself short because you are human."

"My penance," she whispered.

"You started Butterfly House because of her, didn't you?"

"I had to do something or go crazy. She wouldn't let me help her. Oh, Sam, she wouldn't help herself. I couldn't go back there. I thought about sneaking back and trying to convince her, but I couldn't get within two blocks of home without feeling sick to my stomach."

"Then this relationship you spoke of…"

"Classic pattern. Steve seemed wonderful at first, and I was young and alone. And then I started losing myself bit by bit, molded into what he wanted. I became a carbon copy of my mother until the day he hit me and then took my picture and stuck it on the fridge so I would remember what would happen if I put a toe out of line. That was my moment. I packed my things and walked away."

She'd conquered the demon by getting her degree in social work and proving time and again that she was stronger than the fear. But all the while she knew in her heart she was a coward. An imposter.

"I'm going to tell you something and I want you to think about it, Angela." He squeezed her fingers. "What you did back then made today possible. Every decision you've made brought you to this day, in this place, and put you in the position to give help when she finally decided to seek it."

"I want to believe you." It sounded so good, so logical, so exonerating. But was it true?

"You can't force someone to do what they don't have the strength to do. You can't force them to feel what you want them to feel. What you can do is be ready, so that when the day comes, you're there with open arms."

That sounded to Angela like the voice of experience. Sam was thirty-seven. Had he been waiting for someone to come to their senses all this time?

"And who are you waiting for, Sam? Who broke your trust?"

For a long moment he looked into her eyes, as if deliberating whether to speak. Finally he relaxed a little, his lips curving just the tiniest bit. "I'm not waiting for anyone."

And that was where he stopped. All kisses and tender moments aside, he finished his sentence there and said no more. Angela had turned to him tonight because she'd needed him. And he was there because they were…what exactly? More than friends? But he'd had chances to kiss her tonight and the closest he'd gotten was a peck on the forehead, like a brother might give a sister. She'd screwed it up big-time at Diamondback when she ran away.

Because she'd lied. She did want him. She did care and the truly astonishing thing was that she trusted him. With anything. With her life. And she could tell him so or she could let him walk out the door.

CHAPTER ELEVEN

WHEN Angela woke, sun was streaming through the kitchen windows. The throw from the back of the sofa was soft against her skin and a cushion had been placed beneath her head. She felt as though a weight had been lifted even though she knew there was so much heartache to come. But it was going to get better. She just knew it.

She rolled slightly and looked toward the kitchen. Sam. He was standing at the counter in front of the coffeemaker, staring out the window at the backyard as the coffee brewed. Had he slept at all? His jaw was darkened with a layer of stubble and his hair was usually a bit messy so it was hard to tell if he'd slept or not. But she noticed his shirt was now buttoned correctly, and she gave a small smile.

He'd stayed all night. Looked after her in a way no one ever had before. Listened to her, and she'd opened up and let him see all the dark, hidden corners. And yet here he was, making coffee, humming tunelessly, completely oblivious to the changes he'd wrought in her.

She would be okay. She'd be more than okay and so would her mom. Because they would face what needed facing and she wouldn't be afraid.

She shifted on the sofa and he turned and smiled. The sight of him grinning at her made her warm all over, and if the wattage of his smile missed any spot, his easy greeting found the shadows. "Hey, sleepyhead."

Oh, my. Sam's morning voice was husky with the rasp of sleep. "Hey yourself," she replied, trying to keep her pulse under control. "How long have I slept?"

"A few hours. We were talking and then I looked down and you were out like a light."

The idea of falling asleep curled up against his side made her feel all hot and tingly. "Sorry about that."

"Don't be." The coffeemaker beeped and he held up an empty mug. "Want some?"

She pushed herself up to sit, leaving the blanket over her bare legs. He was trying to keep things easy and she needed to follow his lead, even if she was feeling a bit shaky. She didn't quite trust it, but had to admit it felt amazing to let someone look after her for a change. She smiled up at him. "Love some. Black's fine."

He brought her a cup along with one of his own and sat down. "I thought you'd want to know right away that I heard from Mike. They picked up your dad just south of Leduc. He was hitchhiking, on his way here."

She sipped her coffee, trying to sort out her feelings. Relief, certainly, that Jack would not show up. Hope that Beverly was truly on the road to a new life. And simple sadness. This was what her family was reduced to. And it was a mess. It would be for a long time, until things with both her parents got sorted. It certainly wasn't fair to drag Sam into it. He'd done enough last night.

"Mike wants to see you and your mom this morning. They need to interview you both if they're going to press charges. He can only stay in the drunk tank for so long before they have to release him."

"I know." She would face this—face him—after all this time. She had to.

"I can go with you if you want."

The offer was unexpected and generous but unsettling. She knew he was trying to help but couldn't escape the fear of being smothered by his involvement. She ran her finger around the rim of her cup. Didn't he trust her to see it through? She had needed him last night, but she was made of stern stuff. She stopped circling her finger and looked up at him. "To make sure I go through with it?"

He frowned. "Of course not. For support. I know this is going to be very difficult and painful."

Her hands felt cold and she curled them around the heat of the cup. "You're a strong person, Sam. You see a problem and you fix it. You aren't afraid of anything. And it would be easy for me to let you fix this for me, but if last night showed me anything, it's that I need to fix it for myself."

"I wasn't planning on fixing it for you." He sounded put out about it. "It was for moral support, but if you don't want me to go, I won't."

The gap that had narrowed last night started to widen again.

He put his cup down on the table and then took hers and put it down as well. He clasped her fingers in his hands and met her eyes. "But for the record, I do get afraid now and again. I'm not always as strong as I should be."

She doubted it. He was so very perfect, so masculine and approachable with his chocolate eyes and hint of stubble and wrinkled shirt. It wasn't fair that she should find him so attractive when she needed to gather the wherewithal to keep her distance. It would be too easy to let him take the lead.

At that moment Morris jumped up on the couch, stepped carefully across the cushion and curled up on Sam's lap. He started purring instantly while Sam's surprised gaze met hers.

"Well, I'll be," he murmured, letting go of one

of her hands and dropping his to stroke the soft orange fur.

He'd won over Morris. Her timid, cranky boy hadn't just accepted a touch but had sought it out. He hardly ever sat in her lap, let alone curled up in a contented ball. And here he was cuddling with Sam. Traitor.

It shouldn't have irritated her but it did, adding to her sense of feeling alone. She was used to being the one who made things happen, but when it counted she'd frozen. It all came so easily to Sam. Even Morris seemed to have forsaken her this morning, choosing Sam instead.

Sam rubbed his wide hand down Morris's back. "Will you at least promise to call me if you need anything? Or just let me know how it goes later? I'll be worried."

"I appreciate it, Sam, but there's no need for us to take any more of your time. I know you have your own concerns." She would be strong. She would prove it—first to herself, and then to everyone else who had ever doubted.

"There's every need," he contradicted.

Something in the warm timbre of his voice set off alarm bells. "Why?" she asked, trying to pull her fingers away but he held them fast.

He seemed to consider for a moment, then relaxed as if he'd come to some silent decision. "When this is over, we need to talk."

The bells were ringing madly now. "I don't know if that's a good idea. I need to get my mother settled and there'll be legal matters to sort out...not to mention the running of Butterfly House." Nerves flickered in her voice but she was determined. If she relied on Sam now she would never know if she had it in her to defeat her own demons.

"Angela."

The soft but firm way he said her voice cut off her babbling.

"I understand you need to do this by yourself. I really do. But I will worry about you whether you want me to or not. That's what happens when you love someone."

Oh, no, he hadn't just said it. Hope slammed into her chest quickly, followed by despair. His gaze never left her face and time stood still for just a second as she absorbed the words. No one had ever said them to her before. And she knew Sam well enough that she knew he wouldn't say it if he didn't think he meant it. Hearing the words filled her with a momentary, glorious happiness. It was a revelation to know she was loveable.

But they were both going to be so hurt at the end of all this. He wanted to care for her and shoulder her burdens. And what she needed was someone who could step back and let her fight her own battles. When she'd thought it was only her feelings involved it had been better. But now he'd gone and said it out loud without even hesitating or choking on the words. He couldn't take it back even as a small part of her acknowledged that she didn't really want him to.

"You…" She couldn't bring herself to say it, but she couldn't look away from the honesty and emotion in his eyes. She knew he meant it even before he spoke the confirmation.

"I love you, Angela. You drove me insane the first time we met and you haven't stopped. I didn't know what to do with you and your sharp tongue and tidy little suit. I wanted to throttle you and kiss you senseless at the same time. But then something changed. I kept telling myself my feelings were all wrong and you told me to stay away and I thought that would solve it. But when I heard your voice on the phone last night I was so afraid and I knew. Your past doesn't matter. I love you. I just do."

She was without words. Never in her life had she been the recipient of such a speech. And he meant every word. She didn't doubt that for a second.

He leaned in and touched her lips with his and she felt him tremble beneath her hands. She curled her fingers around the cotton of his shirt and held on, absorbing the taste of him so that she could remember. He was always so unspeakably gentle. So gallant and courteous. And she deserved none of it, because she was letting him kiss her even though she knew in the end she'd turn him away.

Morris got cramped and with a meow of complaint jumped off Sam's lap. Sam slid a few inches closer until their bodies brushed. Angela gave herself this moment to cherish because even though she refused to say the words in return, she knew in her heart that she did love him back. She loved his loyalty and strength and the compassion that he sometimes kept hidden behind his hardworking exterior. The hands that worked the land and branded cows and broke horses were as gentle as a butterfly's touch on her skin. And yet she could not give in to it all the way. Because she would ask things of him that were not fair to ask. Things he could not give. She would ask him to stop being himself, and there was no way she could ask that of anyone.

And perhaps—just perhaps—she was afraid that if she forced him to make a choice between Diamondback and her, it wouldn't be her.

She pulled away from the tender embrace and sighed. "Oh, Sam."

The words were wistful and sad and needed no explanation or elaboration. The betrayed look in his eyes said it all for him. She hadn't said it back. They both knew that his declaration was not the beginning of something but the end.

The moment dragged out until he got to his feet, took a few steps, squared his shoulders and turned back to face her.

"This is why I didn't want to talk right now. You've got too much on your mind, too much you have to focus on. Once the dust has settled…"

"It won't change anything." She folded her hands on her knees and looked up at him. He had done so much for her. She'd needled and accused him of some unjust things and in the end he'd come through, every single time. He deserved better than what she had to offer. He was looking for a wife who would move into the position of chatelaine of the ranch. That was his history and legacy. He needed someone who would put his needs—and Diamondback's—first, and that wasn't her. Because Butterfly House was *her* legacy and it was just getting started. She couldn't do both. And if the last twelve hours had taught her anything, it was that she had a lot of work left to do—both personally and professionally. She wasn't ready for what a committed relationship would mean.

"So you don't love me," he said, challenging her.

Could she lie? Could she look him in the eye and say *No, I don't love you, Sam*? She couldn't do it. He would see right through her.

"Where do you see this going?" she asked instead. It was an important question. A flicker of hope still burned. There was a chance she was wrong, after all, a chance that he might say the sorts of words that would give them a chance.

He came closer and squatted down in front of

her, the denim of his jeans stretching taut across his long legs. She longed to reach out and lay her hands on his knees, just to feel connected to him again. She clenched her fingers tighter together to keep from doing it. She had to be strong.

"I saw you at the ranch the night of the open house, remember? You and Clara and mom all together in the kitchen, laughing. It felt so right, Ang. It's never been that way before. For a long time now it's been like living in black and white. And then you walked in and everything was in color again. I want you there, with me. I want you to make a life with me. I want us to face those challenges together."

Angela could think of a half dozen women who would give their right arms to hear such a speech from Sam. What he had to offer any woman was a fine life. A beautiful, stable home, a prosperous living, and an incredible man capable of a lot of love. It was a dream come true. Except it was his dream and not hers.

She shrank back against the cushions. She was horribly afraid that if she said yes she'd end up losing the very best part of herself in the process, making them both miserable. They wouldn't make it. While she knew that Sam would never mistreat her the way Jack and Steve had, she was terribly afraid of losing the part of her she was just beginning to find.

In the end losing Sam would be so much worse than leaving Steve. That hadn't been about love at all. But Sam—he was unfailingly honest and deserved someone who could be as open with him. This time her heart was well and truly involved.

"I'm sorry, Sam. Your life is Diamondback. And mine is not. And that leaves us at a bit of an impasse."

He stood up, looked down at her and made her feel very small. "You'd have me walk away from the ranch?"

"Of course not. Diamondback is who you are. That's what I'm saying, you see?" She couldn't stand being on the sofa anymore and got up, letting the blanket drop to the floor. "You have built your life there. You are a part of the ranch and it is part of you. You need someone to be there by your side, to have a big family. I know you want that; I can see it every time you speak of your parents or your cousin. Family will always be at the center of your life—it's what drives you. And this foundation drives me, don't you see? You can't imagine walking away from the ranch so you must understand how it would be for me to walk away from this."

"You could still help," he offered. "You wouldn't have to give it up." But he looked away, knowing it was a paltry solution next to the absolute truth she spoke.

"I've dreamed of this foundation for most of my life," she said quietly. "If I walk away from this now, I leave the best part of me behind. I leave behind the part that makes me *me*. If you love me at all…"

"You know I do."

Her heart thudded. This was so hard. "If you love me at all," she continued, "you love me because of this place. Because of who it makes me. Because of who it will allow me to become. What is left if you take that away?"

"I would never want you to change who you are!" His eyes blazed at her. "You know that."

"I know you wouldn't mean to. But I have plans. It hasn't ended because of my mother, you know. Yes, I'm hoping this provides us with some healing and closure, but I believe in this project more than ever. I still want to expand and open up other shelters. And you need a wife who won't be traveling around all the time putting something else ahead of you. That's no way to run a relationship. I'd hurt you in the end, Sam, and that's not fair to either of us."

A door opened and shut and shuffling footsteps echoed in the hall. Beverly appeared in the doorway of the kitchen and Angela's heart hurt just looking at her. Dressed in an old nightie and a borrowed housecoat, she looked old and stooped and the fresh wounds on her face had deepened, giving her a tired, battered appearance.

"Mom. I hope we didn't wake you."

"I smelled coffee." The woman tried to smile but her cracked lip started to split and halted the smile in mid curve. Instead she moved to the coffeemaker and took a mug from a hook on a cup tree.

"I can't deal with this right now," Angela whispered to Sam, not sure if she was relieved by the interruption or not. Once he was gone it would truly be over. But sending him away was as close to breaking her heart as she'd ever come and she wasn't sure she was prepared for it. A part of her wanted to put it off as long as she could.

"Of course," he answered, but she detected a chill in his voice that hadn't been there before. Perhaps he was accepting the truth in what she said. It was an impossible choice for either of them to make. She was glad now that she hadn't said the words back to him. It would have made this even more unbearable.

"Mike will be expecting you at his office later this morning. And perhaps you can tell Clara that we can manage today without her. You need her more."

He grabbed his keys from the table and nodded at Beverly while Angela looked on helplessly.

"Mrs. Beck," he said, "I'm Sam Diamond. If you need anything, my family's here to help. Angela's going to take really good care of you. You can trust her to do the right thing."

Oh, the sting in those words, especially now that doing the right thing was costing them both so much. She blinked back tears and walked him to the door.

He paused for a moment on the steps, putting his hands in his pockets. Angela held on to the edge of the door, putting off shutting it, knowing it meant goodbye. Finally he looked up.

"You won't reconsider?"

She swallowed. "I can't," she whispered, looking down at her feet so he wouldn't see the glistening in her eyes.

"I want you to know that I meant what I just said to your mother. Same goes for you. If you ever need anything, I'm a phone call away. Got it?"

She nodded dumbly, still unable to look up at him. Her willpower was hanging by a thin thread. "I've got it."

He spun and jogged down the steps to his truck. Angela shut the door and locked it, then leaned her back against it. She couldn't bear to watch him drive away this time.

Virgil was sitting in the late-August sun, a magazine in his lap. He hadn't even turned the cover. Instead Sam found him staring out over the pasture. Sam followed the path of his gaze and took a deep breath. Angela was right. This was more than home. Diamondback was something he felt through the soles of his feet straight to his heart. He and Virgil both did. And because of their love for the ranch, Sam was determined to give it one last try. There had to be a way to bring his vision for the future and the family all together.

"Dad."

Virgil started at the sound of his voice and Sam smiled wistfully. His father was improving slowly but there was no denying how much he'd aged since his stroke.

He pulled up a chair and sat beside his father. "Where's Clara?"

"Told her I wanted to sit outside for a while. No more fluttering."

Sam chuckled. Virgil's speech was improving, still slow but with fewer slurs. "She's good for you."

"Gives your mother a break. And she's a good woman." Virgil threw Sam a meaningful glance.

"Sorry, Dad. Barking up the wrong tree."

"I know." Virgil nodded. "You and Angela."

Surprise made Sam's mouth drop open. "How did you…"

"I see things. Slow. Not blind."

Sam sat back in his chair. Had he been treating his father as if he was blind? Had he underesti- mated how sharp his father's mind remained while his body betrayed him? He blew out a breath. "Of course. I'm sorry, Dad."

"I know that, too."

The dry August breeze blew across their faces, bringing with it the smell of fresh-cut grass and manure and the hundred other aromas of a ranch at its seasonal peak. For a few minutes Sam was quiet, gathering the words he needed. Hoping that this last time he could break through and make his father understand.

"Dad, I need to say something and I want you to hear me out. Without jumping all over me." Virgil gave him a skeptical look and Sam's lip curved a little. "Okay, at least wait until I'm done."

"Say your piece."

He took a breath. "I think you're afraid, Dad. I think you hate what's happened and you're frustrated and you feel like you're losing control." Virgil's eyes blazed but Sam pressed on. "I think it has got to be hell on earth having to let go of your life's work and I think the fights we've had this summer have been a way for you to make sure you are not forgotten. That you are still a vital piece of Diamondback."

Virgil remained silent. Sam took that as a good sign, an affirmation without Virgil having to say the words.

Encouraged, he leaned forward. "Dad, you *are* Diamondback. I know it's been in the family for generations but you are the one who built it into what it is today. You are the one who took chances and became a leader in this industry. You are the fearless one. And it kills me to see that fearlessness taken away. I don't want to be the one to do it."

A magpie chattered beneath the caragana bushes and Sam watched it bob awkwardly along the grass, weighted down by its cumbersome tail. "I could never cut you out of Diamondback. I want us to do this together. And I know in my heart that this is the right thing. The right thing for right now and the right thing for the generations to come."

"What generations? Don't see any wives or babies runnin' around here."

Sam crossed an ankle over his knee. "Not for lack of trying, okay?" Irritation clouded his voice. The truth was, he hadn't been able to stop thinking about Angela. The bits and pieces he'd got from Clara over the past weeks were paltry crumbs. It had taken all his willpower to let Angela handle the changes in her life on her own, but he'd done it. Because he knew she needed to, for herself.

Besides, she hadn't even said she loved him. And that drove him crazy, because he could see her here, by his side. See their children running around in the hayfields. See himself teaching his son or daughter how to drive a tractor, ride a horse. For years he'd viewed children as a practical necessity, but not now. For the first time ever he could see it all and it wasn't his for the taking.

"You ask her?" Virgil reached out and touched Sam's arm. "Can't say yes if you don't ask."

"I told her I loved her. But it didn't make any difference."

Virgil started laughing. It was wheezy at first, rusty-sounding, and after a few moments he coughed, gasping for air. Sam started to feel alarmed once he got over the shock of seeing Virgil laugh. But Virgil grinned, sat back in his chair and sighed, catching his wind.

"Son, you can be so smart. And so stupid." He took a deep breath, unused to speaking so much. "What's really important here? You pestered me all summer like a dog with a bone. Now at the first sign of trouble with a woman, you run away with your tail between your legs."

"My tail!" Sam burned with indignation. "You don't know, Dad."

"I know enough. I know you gave up. Sad excuse for a Diamond."

Dammit. Sam hated to admit it but Virgil was right. He had given up. Angela had sent him away and he'd let her. He never wanted to seem pushy or overbearing because of her past. But the truth was, he'd been ornery before he knew anything of her history and she'd risen to the challenge, not cowered.

If anything, he'd let her down by not showing her how a man should stand by a woman.

"This project appears to be more important to you anyway," Virgil remarked. "So maybe it's best."

Sam sat back in his chair. He knew exactly what his father was doing and wanted to call him on it. But the truth was smack between his eyes. He'd fought for this but he hadn't fought for her. He thought back over all the reasons he'd just given his father for fighting the ranch development, and realized he could have been speaking to Angela about Butterfly House. She *was* afraid. She had been the one to realize her dream and now she was terrified of losing control. Of losing the most vital part of herself. She'd said it and he hadn't been listening.

"Sam, I'll sign the papers if you want me to. I know you'll do right by Diamondback. But I want you to remember something. This place—this life—means nothing without your mother. Make sure you make the right decisions and for the right reasons."

Virgil was giving Sam all he'd wanted and the victory felt hollow. What stretched before him was a cutting-edge, prosperous future and an empty one. It had taken him thirty-seven years to fall in love and he knew it was going to stick. So what was he going to do about it? Let her go without a fight? Spend the rest of his days at Diamondback, a man of property but with a hole in his soul?

He got up and put his hand on Virgil's shoulder. "Appears I have some thinking to do."

Virgil nodded. "Yessir."

"I'll send Clara out if you like."

"I don't mind sitting a little longer."

Sam gave the shoulder a squeeze before heading inside. An idea was beginning to form, the seedlings of a plan to bring the family together *and* have the woman he loved. Virgil wouldn't like it, but it might just get him the daughter-in-law and grandkids he'd been harping about for years.

CHAPTER TWELVE

THE house seemed horribly quiet. The Cadence Creek Rodeo was on and Clara and the other girls had gone to enjoy the festivities, including entering their own pot of chili in the chili cook-off. It had been a bright spot, seeing the women come out of their shells as they got further acquainted. Angela had heard them giggling over the chili-making, speculating on how many employers they could entice with their secret ingredients.

Angela felt lonely listening to them. She was on the outside yet again and by her own choice. They'd invited Angela along, but she wanted the time alone. Moments of quiet were fewer and farther between these days and she was seldom in the mood for company.

A week had passed since Beverly had moved to a different shelter in another town. While Butterfly House helped women ready to start over, the assistance Beverly needed was different. And as much as Angela wished she could help her mother all on her own, she was wise enough to know she couldn't be objective. Leaving Beverly in someone else's care had been very, very hard. But wounds were healing. They'd hugged and cried a little as Angela had promised to be back to visit soon.

She wished she could say the same about Sam, but she hadn't spoken to him. The only time she'd seen him was when Jane had invited her to go along to church one Sunday. Sam and Molly were in the fourth pew from the front and she'd caught her breath at the sight of him in dress pants and a freshly pressed white shirt, open at the collar, his face smooth from a recent shave but with his hair still the same sexy, unruly mess.

She hadn't gone back to church the next Sunday.

So this afternoon she was spending the afternoon cleaning her room and listening to Patsy Cline. The wistful music suited her mood perfectly. She'd gotten what she wanted, hadn't she? So why did she feel so empty? Maybe it was time to start looking into the next project, scout new locations.

And then Sam's words came back to haunt her. That once he met a challenge he got bored and moved on to another. Was that what she was doing? Except instead of boredom she was running away from her problems.

She didn't have a magic solution, so she put her energies into the job at hand. Her sheets were on the clothesline and she was dusting off her dresser when his voice behind her scared her out of her skin.

"Busy?"

She nearly threw the duster at him as he laughed. Her heart raced from the shock. She'd been thinking about finally decorating this room and listening to Patsy singing about "Walkin' after Midnight" and then there he was. "You should know better than to sneak up on a person like that."

"May I come in?"

She lifted an eyebrow. Mercy, he looked good in new jeans and a crisp Western shirt, his customary Stetson atop his head. "You're going to anyway." She flourished the duster. "Go ahead."

Sam stepped inside, as calm as you please, removed his hat and held it in his hands. Her bedroom was the smallest of the six and he seemed to fill it with all his larger-than-life glory. Why did it seem as if nothing had changed? Maybe he'd realized he was wrong about his feelings. Surely if he still thought he was in love with her it would be more awkward, wouldn't it? Instead it felt as if he'd done this hundreds of times before.

He looked around the room. "You didn't decorate this one like the others."

She shrugged. "The money is allocated for the residents. Those rooms had to come first. I've been thinking about it, though…" She let the thought trail off. The truth of it was Butterfly House didn't feel like home. She wasn't sure where that was—or what it would feel like when she got there. But she'd put off decorating a room for herself just the same.

The CD shifted and "Crazy" started playing.

"Nice music choice." Sam waved his hat in the direction of the turntable. "My mother would approve. She loves Patsy Cline. Bit melancholy for a summer afternoon though, isn't it?"

"There's never a bad time for Patsy," Angela replied, putting down the duster and ignoring his observation about her state of mind. "Are you going to make me ask why you're here, Sam? Is this official Butterfly House board business? Because I figured you'd be at the fairgrounds with everyone else in town."

"I was, for a while." That explained his "dress" Western clothes, then. "My cousin's retiring after this season. But bull-riding's the last event of the day and he's not up for a few hours yet. I ran into Clara and the ladies in the church tent surrounded by Cadence Creek's finest chili. They told me you were stuck at home."

She'd stayed home because the thought of running into him at the rodeo put knots in her belly. Avoiding him wasn't the answer, but she figured one day it would get easier.

"That still doesn't tell me why you're here."

For a long moment he seemed to consider. Finally he said, "How's your mom?"

It touched her that he asked that first thing. "She's doing okay. We filed a report with Mike, and she's in a different place now getting the help she needs. The court date isn't going to be much fun, but we're going to be there together." She smiled a little. "She's going to be okay, and that's the main thing."

"And you? Are you okay?"

"I'm getting there." The truth was she couldn't have done this without his help that first day. It wasn't a magic solution, but she was working on making peace with things. With people.

The music changed, and the opening notes to "I Fall to Pieces" filled the room. Slowly Sam took a step forward, then another. He put his hat back on his head and held out his hand. "Care to? Since you're missing the festivities?"

"Sam…"

"Please, Angela. I've worked myself up to coming here all day and you're not making this easy. Dance with me."

She only complied because she knew how difficult it had been doing without him the last while and didn't want to make it any worse for Sam. She stepped tentatively into his arms, placing one hand in his and the other on his broad muscled shoulder. His hand rested firmly on her waist as he pulled her close. In the tiny floor space his feet shuffled in small steps, but it was enough that she felt the movement of his thighs against hers, the rise and fall of his chest as he breathed, the warmth of his lips next to her hair that was shoved carelessly in a ratty ponytail.

"I'm sorry." He whispered it next to her ear, sending shivers down her spine as they swayed to the music.

It was not what she'd been expecting. "What do you have to be sorry about?"

"That I gave up."

"I told you to, remember?" Her heart started beating abnormally. She'd been the one to send him away. And she'd been the one to cry into her pillow at night because of it. Her reasons had been right, so why had it felt so wrong?

"You were scared and you should have had a friend by your side. Not to go through it for you, but with you. Instead I let you push me away, and I'm sorry I wasn't stronger."

Her lip quivered. "You scare me, Sam. You make me doubt everything."

"Why?"

His feet stopped moving for a moment and he drew back, looking down into her eyes. She gathered courage, knowing she'd faced her demons alone and she'd been strong enough to do it, but that she'd also missed him every moment. She'd been very wrong to push him away when she should have trusted him. "Because of the intensity I feel when I'm with you. I'm so afraid of getting lost in it."

"I know you are."

"You do?" She looked up at him with surprise. He hadn't understood before. He'd had his eye on a perfect Diamondback life where she could "help" with the Butterfly Foundation. The fact that she'd been at all tempted still frightened her to death. Was she so weak that she'd trade in her dream so easily?

"Of course I do. When you open yourself up to someone, then you allow them the opportunity to hurt you. To disappoint you. And you've already been hurt enough, sweetheart."

His feet started moving again, but slower, and she had the weirdest sensation that they were snuggling. He'd called her sweetheart again, she realized with a sigh. And despite trying to hold her feelings inside, she knew that she'd shared things with Sam already that she'd never shared before with another person. She trusted him, believed in his goodness. That was a brand-new feeling.

"By the way—Dad signed off on the biogas project."

She furrowed her brow, confused at the abrupt change of subject but willing to follow along if it meant she could stay within the circle of his arms. "How did you convince him to do that?"

"I was honest with him. I finally realized that he was afraid of being invisible, afraid of losing all he'd worked so hard to build. Holding out was the one thing he could still control when everything else was flying to pieces. But I told him that he would never be unimportant or ignored. Because we're in it together. That's what people who love each other do, you know?"

"No, Sam. I never had a family like yours so I don't know."

But he persisted. "I think you do. Look at what you've done for your mother. You are standing beside her even though she hurt you. You do the right thing, Angela, always. You give people a voice who otherwise don't have one. And yet your voice goes unheard."

Their feet stopped and her throat swelled. How could he see all of that? How could he know? She stumbled back, out of his arms, but he caught her fingers and held on.

"I didn't hear you." He captured her gaze and held it. "I didn't listen to what you were saying. It wasn't until I understood my dad that I got it."

He reached over and cupped her cheek. "You're a butterfly that needs to fly, not be shut up in a jar somewhere. I hear you now," he said softly, "and it's high time someone fought for you. I love you so much, Angela. And I was a fool to let you push me away. I told you the morning after your mother arrived, do you remember? That you can't force someone to feel what you want them to feel. What you can do is be ready, so that when the day comes, you're there with open arms." His forehead touched hers. "My arms are open now, Ang. Hoping you're ready."

The floodwaters broke and she went into his embrace. Oh, he felt so good, so strong, so right. His shirt smelled like detergent and the outdoors and the spicy scent that was distinctly Sam. "I love you, too," she said, her voice muffled against the cotton.

This man—this gorgeous, humbling, incredible man before her—was offering her the moon. How could she not take it? As her eyesight blurred through her tears she realized that surrendering to her feelings only made her more, not less. That over the last few difficult weeks she'd wanted him by her side not to bear the burden for her but to share it with her. Somehow, by some miracle, he'd restored her faith.

She leaned back and laid her hand on his tanned cheek. "I do love you, and it's hurt me so much to hold it inside."

"I never wanted to hurt you." He put his hand over hers, holding it there against the warmth of his skin, turning his head a little so he could kiss the base of her palm. His eyes closed for a second and his thick lashes lay against his cheek. Angela was swamped by a love so whole, so complete, she knew she'd remember this moment forever.

"I know that," she whispered, and he opened his eyes.

"I have a plan," he said. "Would you hear it? Please?"

Staying away from him hadn't solved a thing; she'd been utterly miserable. Besides, Sam wasn't the kind of man who said please often. He was used to having his own way. He was the kind of man who took charge rather than be at anyone's mercy. And that strong, forceful man was holding her in his arms saying please. Hope glimmered as she nodded just the tiniest bit, encouraging him to go on.

"I spent my whole life focusing on Diamondback. It meant everything to my mom and dad and then to me, too. It defined the Diamond family. I remember when times were tight. How we were looked down upon rather than up to. When things started to change, when the years of careful management paid off, I got cynical."

He squeezed her fingers. "I'm getting to the romantic part, I promise. I saw the love between my parents and knew I could never settle for anything less than the example they set. No one ever measured up—until I met you. Angela…"

Oh, lord. His dark eyes were wide and earnest and her heart was pattering a mile a minute.

"You really don't know, do you?" A soft smile touched his lips. "You walked into that benefit and it was like someone hit me right here and stole my breath." He pressed a hand to the middle of his chest. "And when you get talking numbers and figures and demographics it's a sight to behold. But it's not just that, either. You're compassionate, and strong."

She swallowed past the tears thickening her throat. But he wasn't done yet.

"And then I thought maybe you did care for me. I could see our life together. But it was still about me. It wasn't until I talked to Dad that I truly understood. He said something to me that day that brought it all back to one. He said that Diamondback and his life would have been nothing without Mom. And I realized he was right. I've been miserable. I holler at people and spend too much time brooding in the barn. I'm no quitter but I'd given up on us. I had to be willing to fight for us. And that meant putting us first. The only way to do that is to share your dreams with you. Because Diamondback be damned, Ang." His dark eyes shone down at her. "My dream is you. The rest of it doesn't matter if I don't have you."

He lifted her hand to his lips and kissed it, the gesture so chivalrous and tender that if she hadn't before, Angela would have lost her heart completely.

"I was looking for a way to put my family back

together, and I couldn't see that you are doing it just by being you."

"I am?"

He nodded. "You made me see things from my dad's side. You helped my mom ask for help, became her friend. The only thing missing now is Ty—he belongs home rather than roaming the country. And now even he has a reason to come back."

"He does?" She was trying hard to keep up, but she couldn't see how she'd had anything to do with Sam's cousin whom she'd never met.

"I'm asking you to compromise," he said. "Make Diamondback the home base for something extraordinary. You don't belong running one single house, Angela, you deserve to be heading up the whole foundation. Hire a director for here, and oversee the start-up of each and every house built to help those who need it. I don't want you to give up your dreams. I want to share them with you, be with you every step of the way. And I hope that in the end, you'll share mine. Make a home with me at Diamondback. Maybe raise a family. A ranch is a good place to have kids. Hard work and open spaces and two parents who love and respect each other."

"You want to marry me. And have babies." Her mind was spinning, with the words he was saying tumbling about like little miracles and bubbles of possibilities she hadn't even considered before.

He tucked a piece of hair behind her ear, smiling

softly. "Yes, I want to marry you." He grinned. "And have babies. Maybe I'm not great with teenagers but I'm guessing I'll learn, especially with you there beside me. What will it take to convince you?"

The CD had long since run out and the room echoed with expectant silence.

"I know you want to make this happen, but, Sam, you can't be gone from the ranch all the time and your father is in no shape to go back to work." She wanted to believe him. Wanted it desperately.

"This is the best part. My cousin is retiring and coming home to run Diamondback with me. A full partnership. That means that I don't have to be at the ranch 24/7. I know that I can go away from time to time and the ranch is in good hands. It's where he's belonged all along anyway. The family all together."

"Your cousin?" she asked. "But I thought he was estranged from the family."

Sam grinned. "Convincing him to come back wasn't easy. He and Dad haven't seen eye to eye in a long time. Peas in a pod, that's why if you ask me. But Ty's sharp and he's a hard worker. If it hadn't been for one big blow-up I don't think he'd have gone in the first place. Even so, it took my trump card to make him say yes."

She risked a smile. "Of course you have an ace up your sleeve. You always do."

His lips curled in a sexy, private smile. "A long time ago we made a pact that we'd never lose our heads over a woman. I told him I had fallen in love and wouldn't have as much time to dedicate to the ranch. He said he didn't believe it and that it was something he needed to see in person. But it's just an excuse. I think he knows it's time he came home."

Sam had turned his life upside-down to make this happen. All for her. It was everything she wanted and it made her want to weep.

She put her hand on his chest and tipped her face up to his. "I had to face some things on my own, had to prove to myself that I was strong enough to be me and come out of the shadow that's been hanging over me for so long. But I missed you the whole time, Sam. I wish I could have done that without sending you away. I don't feel like I deserve you. I asked too much, I…"

"Hush." He placed a finger over her lips. "You taught me that it's about what you give, rather than what you get. You deserve far more than you think, and I'm going to spend my life showing you—if you'll say yes."

There was no other possible answer to give. He was offering her everything—the Butterfly Foundation, a home, brown-eyed and dark-haired babies to call her Mama. She just had to be brave enough to trust, and believe and reach out and grab it.

She cupped his face in her hands and kissed his lips. "Yes," she whispered. "Yes."

EPILOGUE

THE fall day was gilded in hues of gold—the ripe harvests in the field, the drying grasses in the meadows, the gold coin-shaped leaves rustling on the poplar trees. The guests sat in rented chairs on the lawn while Sam stood at the top of the newly painted porch, where he'd shared lemonade and those first confidences with Angela in the twilight.

Sam watched as she made her way up the path, walking slowly in a simple white dress with her hand on Virgil's arm as he took small steps behind a rolling walker. When they'd announced their engagement, Virgil had insisted on walking her down the "aisle," and he and Clara had kept it a secret as they'd worked over the past weeks. Sam's throat thickened at the sight and he ran a finger between his neck and the tight collar of his new shirt. Angela smiled up at him and the world stopped. It was just the two of them now as she took the steps with her small train gliding behind, the long veil floating in the fall breeze.

"I, Samuel, take you, Angela..."

"I, Angela, take you, Samuel..."

She smiled at the use of his full name and he smiled back, full of a happiness he hadn't known existed. Within minutes it was done—the ring was on his finger where he planned to keep it forever.

The reception was held at Diamondback in a huge tent set up in the garden. The asters, chrysanthemums and dahlias were still blooming, their spicy scents mixed with the delectable smell of Diamondback's finest prime rib.

Clara, Angela's only bridesmaid, came to offer her last congratulations before taking Virgil inside after the excitement of the day.

"I'm going in now, but I wanted to say happy wedding day to you both." She gave Angela a quick hug. "I'm going to miss you around the house, but you're going to have a wonderful time."

Sam had booked them in a chalet in Quebec's Eastern Townships for a week's honeymoon, to be followed by a week in Ottawa where they'd be in meetings about federal funding for the Butterfly Foundation. A new director of the Cadence Creek house had been hired, and a temporary office had already been set up at Diamondback for Angela to use until construction finished on their new house. He intended to keep his promises.

Sam hugged Clara as well—she'd gotten over her physical shyness with him shortly after their engagement. "Have you met Ty yet?" he asked. "Your paths will be crossing a lot from now on as he'll be staying in the house. Hang on."

He waved his cousin over. "Ty, come on over here."

Ty looked out of place in his suit. His jaw sported a faint bit of stubble and the suit coat hung awkwardly on his rangy frame. Sam hid a smile. Ty was back but he was still determined to do things his way. Thankfully that didn't mean butting heads with each other. But Sam had his doubts where Virgil was concerned. Ty and Virgil seemed to set each other off without trying. The next few months would be interesting. Still, he was convinced they'd work through it.

"Ty, this is Dad's assistant, Clara."

"Mr. Diamond," she said, and Sam saw the defiant set of her jaw as she held out her hand. It was more than she'd done with him at their first meeting, and Sam shared a look with his new wife. It was good progress.

"It's just Ty," he replied, taking her hand and shaking it. Sam saw Clara's eyes widen at the contact before she pulled her hand away. "Or Tyson if I'm on your bad side."

"Right. Well, I'd better get your dad inside. Goodnight everyone."

When she was gone, Sam saw Ty's gaze following her to the house.

"Go easy," Sam warned.

"Did I do anything?" There was a hint of belligerence in Ty's voice. Boy, he did still have a chip on his shoulder.

"Of course not," Angela stepped in with a smile. "Clara was our first Butterfly House resident, that's all. Sam just wants you to respect that."

Ty's gaze narrowed as he watched Clara's sage-green skirt disappear through the deck door. "Her husband abused her?"

"They weren't married, but yes," Angela confirmed. "But we know you'll be considerate, Ty. Don't worry."

Ty hesitated a moment, then to Sam's surprise excused himself and started toward the house.

Sam started forward but Angela stopped him with a hand on his arm. "Let him go. She'll put him in his place if need be. I'm not worried, Sam. Ty's a good man underneath all his cockiness." She grinned. "Like his cousin."

"Like your husband," he corrected, pulling her into his arms.

"Don't worry," she said, standing up on tiptoe and touching her lips to his. "I know how lucky I am. There's no other Diamond like you, Sam."

"Damn right," he confirmed, and picked her up, spinning her in a circle of happiness.

* * * * *